THE G-BOMB

The cleverest man on Earth, Jonas Glebe, becomes the unwitting tool of a baleful intelligence. His invention, the G-Bomb, should bring riches to himself and his daughter Margaret — instead it brings death and a deadly threat to mankind . . . Val Turner knows the danger, but he's imprisoned — framed for Margaret's murder. His release comes too late to prevent the cataclysm engulfing the world. But fate decrees that he saves a strange little man from drowning, and thereby changes destiny . . .

JOHN RUSSELL FEARN

THE G-BOMB

Complete and Unabridged

LINFORD
Leicester

First published in Great Britain

First Linford Edition
published 2010

British Library CIP Data

Fearn, John Russell, *1908 – 1960.*
   The G-Bomb. - - (Linford mystery library)
   1. Science fiction.
   2. Large type books.
   I. Title II. Series
   823.9'12–dc22

   ISBN 978–1–44480–420–1

Published by
F. A. Thorpe (Publishing)
Anstey, Leicestershire

Set by Words & Graphics Ltd.
Anstey, Leicestershire
Printed and bound in Great Britain by
T. J. International Ltd., Padstow, Cornwall

This book is printed on acid-free paper

1

Other eyes watching

The crew of the spaceship that had crossed an interstellar gulf was in conference. Recently revived from their long sleep in suspended animation, they were in orbit a million miles from the Earth. Their craft was hidden from any observers on Earth by reason of a projected image that gave it the appearance of a lifeless chunk of rock, just one of many near-Earth objects drifting in space.

Altogether there was a score of them, big-domed, broad-chested beings, accustomed to an attenuated atmosphere and light gravitation. They had voyaged to Earth from their slowly dying home planet, some 100 light-years distant, guided unerringly by a signal sent from a computer-controlled probe craft that had discovered the Earth more than two hundred and fifty years earlier.

'My friends,' their Leader said quietly,

surveying his alien comrades, 'we face an unexpected problem. The race inhabiting this planet are much more numerous and scientifically advanced than was originally reported to us by our robot probe. We did not foresee how they could have developed so quickly.'

'Was the probe in error?' one of the crew asked. 'Has it malfunctioned?'

'No. On the contrary, it has performed perfectly. Its computer brain has been making observations and recordings ever since it arrived. All of its valuable data has now been transferred to our own ship's central computer brain. As Leader, I was revived ahead of the rest of you, and I have been analyzing the recorded data. I now know everything about this planet and its peoples, including its main languages — thanks to computer analysis of their radio and television broadcasts. In their main language, English, they call themselves 'humans' and their planet is known as 'Earth'. They measure time in units of what they call 'years', this being the period of their revolution around their sun. Our probe arrived here some 250 of their years ago.'

A ripple of unease passed amongst the assembled crew. 'They have radio and television? Just how advanced are they?' one of them asked. 'When we set out on this mission, they had neither! The data we had said that they were an extremely backward race, without even any mechanized transport! How has this mistake been made?'

'No mistake has been made.' The Leader spoke irritably. 'The situation has arisen purely because of the limiting factor of the speed of light. On its arrival here, the probe sent a radio signal back to our home world, stating that Earth was a fair world, with a breathable atmosphere and abundant natural resources — ideal for our race to migrate to. Its backward inhabitants were relatively few in number, of no account scientifically, and could easily be eliminated or enslaved. The radio signal took some 100 Earth years to reach our planet. Immediately it was received, our ship was readied as the vanguard for our invasion, our mission being to prepare the way for our race to migrate here. Naturally, since we cannot travel faster than light, we were obliged to go into suspended animation. Allowing for deceleration, it has taken us another 150 Earth years to arrive. But in that interval — whilst we slept in suspended animation — this Earth race has increased its population astronomically by advances in medical science, and advanced at a phenomenal rate, from animal transport to space travel and an atomic age technology!'

'Space travel!' another ripple of unease amongst the crew. 'Are we in danger of detection by Earth vessels?'

'No.' The Leader waved a deprecating tentaculate hand. 'They are still at an early stage, and apart from unmanned probes, have not ventured much beyond their dead satellite. Even if their instruments detect our vessel, they will take it to be just space debris — a chunk of rock. They appear to be obsessed with putting observation satellites into close orbit for spying upon themselves — completely unaware that *we* are spying upon *them!*'

There was a relaxation of tension amongst the crew.

'Another of their traits is to make visual reconstructions of their own past history, with what they call 'films'. They also make other rather ridiculous films that are entirely fictional, which apparently they find entertaining. These films are constantly being broadcast, and many of them have been recorded by our probe. Our central computer was able to select and replay to me those that had genuine historical content. It was these that I found to be immensely useful.' The Leader paused and looked at his fellows, saw that he had their complete attention.

'Once,' he resumed, 'not too long ago, the Earth people came close to completely destroying themselves in a world-wide conflict. Just when it seemed our ambition would be realised, when they developed the atomic bomb, they ceased fighting! At that very supreme moment when it seemed logical they would annihilate each other, they became peaceful, and, for the time being, our cause was lost. There continue to be numerous localised conflicts, but they result in relatively few deaths — at least, for our purposes.'

There was a murmuring of frustration amongst the assembled crew. The Leader clenched a tentaculate hand on a broad table in front of him.

'Our need, my friends, grows more desperate with the passing years. Our home planet is no longer of service. Its surface has become too arid and its air too thin for us to move far from our underground cities and these cities demand a colossal amount of power for their upkeep, far more than we can really afford. Already our race is hampered in expansion because we have deliberately put a limit on the number of matings and progeny we can allow. Such depletion cannot be stopped unless we have again a world whereon we can live in freedom, a world whose surface is bountiful, where the atmosphere is breathable. For many cycles we have been sending exploratory probes to all sectors of space. At the time we left, only one world had been discovered that fitted the description, and that is the one that is called 'Earth' by those who dwell on it. And we were selected to form the vanguard.'

This time the assembled crew merely nodded courteously and then glanced at one another. They did not dare reveal that they were bored, for they certainly were. All this recounting of known facts was tedious. Their chief anxiety was to know what the Leader proposed to do next.

'Our numbers are not sufficient to permit of us invading Earth and conquering it,' the Ruler resumed after a moment. 'Our science is superior, certainly, but if we flung ourselves into an all-out war against Earth and tried to invade it we would be bound to tear great gaps in our ranks. The Earth people are not primitive by any means, and they have weapons that could certainly inflict grievous losses upon us. In our depleted condition we cannot afford that risk. Our best strategy lies in making these Earthlings destroy themselves and so leave us an empty planet, or if not that, then one so denuded that our victory over them would prove superlatively easy. To that end, I have been perfecting a plan whilst I waited for the automatic machines to revive you at their appointed time.' He paused, then added triumphantly: 'I have chosen a weapon which, produced on Earth, should definitely lead certain factions to precipitate that cataclysm that will pave the way for a successful invasion.'

The assembled crew began to take more interest. Apparently they were arriving at the point they wanted — a method of causing the Earth race to destroy itself.

'I am referring to the Gravity-Bomb. Can you imagine the reaction of certain factions on Earth to a weapon like that? I am convinced that such a device, allied to the knowledge of atomic power that they already possess, will lead them to destroy themselves, and our mission will be accomplished.'

'An excellent conception,' one of the alien crew commented, 'but it will call for considerable selection to choose the right people on Earth. No one must ever be suspicious of the other, or the cause will be lost before it begins. They must not have the least idea that they were being manipulated by us.'

'If they did become suspicious what could they do?' the Leader asked, shrugging. 'They are scientific up to a point, but they haven't the least idea that they are being watched by a race of expert scientists who have learned all there is to know of the secrets of radiation and mind-force. They cannot devise a barrier to the mind-emanations we will send forth. Violence amongst them must be fostered to the greatest possible extent. We shall never perpetuate our race to its full glory otherwise. However, come with me now and I will show you those whom I have selected for our plan.'

The Leader rose, and with unhurried dignity, led the way from the chamber, his contemporaries following behind him. They passed down the immaculate, polished corridors of the large vessel, and so finally reached the giant laboratory wherein was housed all the creative genius of the aliens.

At the entrance the Leader glanced behind him at his followers. 'Actual hypnosis en masse, I have found, cannot be used. The law of self-preservation, highly developed in Earthlings, prevents them from absorbing hypnotic orders to kill themselves.'

The Leader led the way to a section of the gigantic laboratory where the astronomical observations were being conducted.

Although they were a million miles above the surface of the planet the huge X-ray devices incorporated in the reflectors penetrated straight through intervening atmosphere and solids as if it were glass. Nor were the telescopic mirrors anything like those on Earth. They worked magnetically, absorbing light-photons and then amplifying them, with the result that images up to millions of miles away were reproduced with almost their original size upon the receiver screen before which the alien expedition now stood.

'First,' the Leader said, touching a button, 'I wish you to see the man who, I trust, will become prime mover in our cosmic chess game. He has been intimately studied, his brain analysed, and his hopes and ambitions clarified. Here he is.'

Under the actuation of countless controls the telescopic equipment picked up a solitary point upon the planet Earth, a million miles away, and there appeared on the screen a pin-sharp image of an elderly man, sixty perhaps, poring over a mass of sketches and scientific notes. In appearance he was nondescript with straggly grey hair, a thin face, and small body. In fact, his general attire and the surroundings amidst which he was working conveyed the impression that he was not too well-blessed with the world's goods.

'His name,' the Leader said, 'is Jonas Glebe. To us a peculiar name: to him, as an Earthling, quite normal. He lives in a country called England in a town — or rather a city — called London. He has one daughter, Margaret, who whilst not possessing any of his scientific tendencies, is nevertheless his bosom companion when she is not engaged on a task that occupies her every day. Apparently, as did the members of our civilisation in the long-dead past. Earth people work daily at some particular task, usually one for which they are neither mentally nor physically fitted, and in return they receive money, the balance of which — after dues to the State and other bodies — they are allowed to retain to keep themselves alive. A curious, archaic mode of existence, my friends.'

The aliens watched the elderly man busy with his papers. Presently they saw

11

him fling them aside in disgust and sit pondering.

'On the dial here,' the Leader said, nodding to it, 'you see recorded his mental-energy quotient. It is not a high one, but finely balanced. Observe — '

The others looked and saw a delicate electro-magnetic needle hovering around a reading that was approximately one third of the highest possible mental rating known to their science and rarely reached even by their master-brains.

'Yes, fairly high,' the Leader repeated, 'and being finely balanced it will be capable of receiving the mental sugges- tions we shall project at him. By profession he is a small-time scientist and has made a little money by means of what the Earthlings call 'gadgets', but he could certainly do with a good deal more. Now, let us suppose that we plant in his brain the secret of the gravity-bomb. He will claim it as his own idea, of course, and endeavour to market it. Since he will not know where to start we shall have to mentally suggest to him that he deals with this person. Observe him — '

Under the manipulation of the telescopic controls the view of Jonas Glebe faded from view and was gradually replaced by one of a man seated in an opulent office. There were six telephones on his enormous desk and behind him was an immense window giving a view over the dreary roofs of London. The man himself was very square-shouldered with iron-grey hair, closely-cut, sensual lips, and rather prominent eyes. In dress he was immaculate and costly rings glittered on his fat fingers as he thumbed through stacks of documents.

'You are looking at Miles Rutter,' the Leader explained. 'I am not sure that is his real name, but in any event he is the second protagonist in our experiment. He is a man of power, tremendous wealth and influence, and under various names controls many enterprises, most of them connected with Earth's basic necessities like metals, food transport lines, and so forth. He has tremendous ambitions. This man Rutter wants the world, like many before him, and he has every conceivable means of achieving his ambition — except one. He has no scientific weapon powerful enough to set fire to the tinder pile. With the G-Bomb, my friends, we can provide the missing factor.'

'Agreed.'

'There,' the Leader said, switching off, 'we have the two main characters. The one with the G-Bomb, and the other with the ruthless ambition necessary to destroy the human race in his effort to dominate it. Nothing could be simpler or, I hope, more certain of success.'

'Who have we on the other side?' one of the expedition asked, as the Leader stood musing amidst the apparatus.

'The other side?'

'Yes. It has always seemed to me that no matter what destroyer a man invents, there is always somebody clever enough to devise a defence. I cannot believe that on this thickly-populated world of Earth there will not be a scientist capable of finding a deterrent to the Gravity-Bomb.'

The Leader smiled. 'You are rating the intelligence of these Earth people extremely high, my friend, which is not at all a sensible procedure. Though we have not, of course, gone through the involved task of testing every Earth mind individually we have at least discovered that the vast majority range around one fifth of our abilities. That is extremely poor. Here and there an exception does touch the thirty percent mark. In Jonas Glebe alone have we found a registration of thirty-five.'

'Which means he is the cleverest man on Earth?'

'Potentially, yes, but even the cleverest man cannot prove his power unless he offers something superbly brilliant — and that is what the G-Bomb will seem to be. Have no fear. There is not a man or woman on Earth capable of finding a neutraliser for the G-Bomb. All we have to do is transmit the details of it, and then watch Earth people gradually set about the task of destroying each other.'

The aliens nodded but asked no further questions. As far as they could see there were none to ask. The fact that a pair of men on Earth were going to become pawns in their game did not concern them in the least. They had long since passed the point where they had any sentiment for living beings, as such. All of them. Even their own people, were but units to be handled as science deemed best.

The Leader crossed to a massive apparatus with a keyboard like the manual of an organ. A switch started a pale emerald beam projecting downwards so that it completely enveloped the Ruler's head. With a gradually deepening dreamy look in his eyes, he sat back, mechanical aids operating the keyboard for him. He concentrated — and the others watched and made no utterance.

★　★　★

It was the click of the door latch that made Jonas Glebe glance up quickly. He blinked, surprised to notice how much the gloom of the winter afternoon had closed in. The small living room was cold and full of grey shadows. Against the solitary window with its faded net curtains the rain was battering relentlessly.

'Why, dad, what on earth's the idea?' Margaret Glebe came into the gloomy room and switched on the light. Her father blinked in the abrupt glare and Margaret, her wet rainproof gleaming, observed him in concern.

'Anything the matter, dad?' She came over to him quickly. 'You're not — not ill or anything?'

'Bless you, dear, no. I was just lost in thought. I sort of forgot everything.'

Margaret gave a little sigh of relief. 'Oh well, if that's all! Y'know, you're a terrible one to look after yourself. Fire's not on, and you were sitting in the dark. Next thing we know you'll be catching bronchitis. Do you realise it's nearly six o'clock? I got home a little earlier this evening: Mary's taking the cash-desk for me.'

'Oh — Six o'clock? Is it?' Jonas Glebe stirred stiffly and squinted at the clock on the mantelshelf. 'I hadn't realised. I suppose one doesn't when thinking.'

'No, dad, I suppose not.' By this time Margaret had pulled off her rainproof and switched the kettle in the adjoining kitchen. She turned to look through the open doorway and said quietly: 'I just wish your thinking did you some good, that's all. You've been at it for years, ever

17

since I was a little girl anyway, and I can't remember how much benefit it brought you beyond a cheque for a gadget maybe.'

Her father was silent, absently studying her. She was good-looking after a fashion — dark, as her mother had been with straight features and a practical chin. She had none of her father's abstractedness, and certainly none of his inner scientific genius. Her present occupation was that of cashier at a cinema: her ambition, to find a young man who could take a load from her shoulders.

'I suppose I am a bit of a nuisance,' her father sighed, getting to his feet.

'Maybe I should have married earlier then you wouldn't have such an old father. I'm pretty much in your way, dear, aren't I?'

'Dad how can you say such a thing!' Margaret kissed him gently, and then gave him a serious look. 'You're never in my way! You've misconstrued what I mean. I think you don't get a just reward for the things you can do. You're one of the best scientists in the country — in the world in fact — and what happens? They say you're too old to join a scientific organization — too old at sixty-two — and your best ideas you forget to patent or something, and somebody else nets a fortune on them whilst you get a pittance. It isn't right, dad. I don't want to sound as though I'm lecturing you, but you ought to wake up.'

'And do what, my dear?'

'Well — something.' Margaret looked vaguely about her. 'Some kind of quiet job perhaps, and do your scientific dabbling in your spare time.'

Jonas Glebe shook his head. 'Believe me, Marg, if I took a job it wouldn't be doing my employer a service, or myself either. I'd be thinking of other things all the time and my paid work would suffer in consequence. No, once you're a scientist there's nothing else you can do properly; not when you get to my age, anyhow. I realise that a job might improve our surroundings, but is that so very important. We're happy, aren't we?'

'Yes, we're happy, but — ' Margaret fell silent, her eyes on the untidy little living room. Then she glanced towards the doors that led to the two small bedrooms.

'A man doesn't need anything more than a roof over his head where he can work out his problems,' Jonas Glebe said. 'A youngster like you needs much more of course, but you have it. You're out all day, and in the evening too if you wish. You don't see much of this flatlet of ours. If you think it worries me, it doesn't. A man can have thoughts which blind him to his surroundings.'

The girl went across to the kettle as it clicked off. Busy with her own thoughts she made the tea, and then set out the table. During the process her gaze travelled to the stacks of notes on the little bureau at which her father invariably worked. She had seen notes like that for as long as she could remember and it assaulted her practical mind that nothing ever seemed to come of them.

'Just what line of thought prompted you to sit in the dark with the electric fire switched off?' she asked, when she and her father were seated at the simple tea.

'That? Oh, I had the dim beginnings of an idea, only I'm not sure whether I should go ahead with it. It's an idea so simple and yet so diabolical I'm almost afraid to speculate further.'

'Simple yet diabolical?' Margaret gave a frown. 'How could it be?'

'It's a bomb,' her father explained simply, buttering a slice of teacake.

'Oh! Don't you think the world's had enough of bombs and slaughter without adding more? Anyway, what else can there be in bombs? We've already got the atomic bomb and the hydrogen bomb. Don't tell me you've thought of one that's even more horrible?'

'No. My bomb has nothing to do with a particular explosive: that could be left to the organisation buying the bomb. It's just an empty case to start with and you can put in it what you like, from plutonium to ordinary gunpowder. Just the same it's — fiendish.'

Margaret puzzled the business out to herself as her father became momentarily silent, musing to himself. Then he stirred a little as he realised his daughter's eyes were upon him.

'It's so tremendously simple,' he said. 'I

can't think why it never occurred to me before — or if not to me then to an inventor of armaments somewhere.'

'You're not being frightfully explicit, dad!'

Jonas Glebe smiled. 'Sorry, dear. That's because I haven't worked out the details. Not much use me claiming I have something wonderful and starting to explain it until I'm sure, is there?'

'Then you do intend to go ahead with this thing, diabolical or otherwise?'

'I think somehow that I should.' Jonas Glebe looked absently in front of him. 'Don't ask me why: just an impulse. After all, even if the notion is diabolical it doesn't say the bomb will ever be used, does it? It might become such a deterrent to war that no one will ever start one again. That would be quite an achievement! That I, Jonas Glebe, should be the man who stopped war.'

Margaret shook her head slowly. 'You're a dreamer, dad, plain and simple. Neither you nor anybody else will ever stop war as long as there are human beings. There'll always be somebody trying to be top dog. If I were you I'd forget all about the idea, and invent something simple — like an automatic teapot which brews and pours itself for instance.'

Jonas Glebe only smiled. He did not comment. The far-away look was back in his eyes and Margaret knew what that meant. She gave up the argument and turned her attention to finishing her tea. After it was over she cleared away, and then departed to her bedroom. Half-an-hour later she reappeared to find her father seated by the fire, figuring industriously.

'Don't mind if I go out, dad?' she asked. 'I've a date with Ted Jackson.'

'By all means!' Her father did not even glance up. He waved an assenting hand and kept his eyes on his calculations. So Margaret departed and, as the evening advanced gradually forgot her scientific father's preoccupation with obscure problems. It looked, when she came home towards eleven, as though he had hardly moved position.

'Ted didn't turn up,' she announced in

disgust drawing off her gloves. 'That's the last date he'll make with me!'

'I've got it, Marg,' her father interrupted. 'Taken me most of the evening to plan it out, but there's little doubt that it will work. I think I'll call it the G-Bomb, partly to honour the first letter of our surname and partly because gravity is its motivating force.'

'Uh-huh,' Margaret acknowledged, again switching the kettle on, seemingly a routine operation, and then removing her coat. She found it difficult to think of bombs when Ted Jackson had failed to keep his date.

'It's quite unique,' her father added, looking up from his pile of sketches and notes. 'Want to hear about it?'

'Yes, but, do you think I'd understand it? I haven't a scientific bone in my body, as you've so often said!'

'You'll understand this, in non-scientific language. You realise, for a start, that one solid blocks another? That is, you can realise that you don't fall through the floor because the floor is a stronger solid than you are?'

'That's plain enough.' Margaret sat down in the battered armchair by the fire and looked absently into the glowing bars. She saw Ted Jackson dancing there. When the image of Ted Jackson had danced into a red haze she became conscious of the click of the kettle and her father's words. ' . . . so of course, with the electronic poles altered the bomb passes through the solid, and there we are.'

'Yes.' Margaret looked at him rather blankly. 'Yes, dad, I see — I think. Excuse me, the kettle — '

'You haven't heard a word I've been saying,' her father said; then he smiled. 'Never mind, I hardly expected it. At your age science doesn't mean a thing to a girl, and romance comes in an easy first, but for your own sake I should try and do better than Ted Jackson. As to myself,' he went on, musing as Margaret filled the teapot, 'I'm wondering how much money we can rake up.'

'Money!' Margaret nearly dropped the kettle. 'For what?'

'The G-Bomb, of course. It won't be

any use me just submitting a sketch to an interested party. He'll want to see what a model can do, so I must make one. It will cost me a few thousand pounds.'

Margaret had finished laying the supper before she passed a comment, during which time her father had been putting the finishing touches to one of the many curious designs he had made.

'We might as well try and rake up a few million, dad,' she said flatly. 'It just can't be done.'

'But it must!' Her father glanced up, full of surprise that his wish couldn't be instantly granted. 'This has got to be completed.'

'Yes dad, I daresay — and you're an old darling — but I do feel bound to tell you that up till now your inventions have cost us several thousand pounds with a total net return of something like half your expenditure! That's bad business in any language. We could well do with that lost money. We wouldn't be in this dump if we had it.'

'So you're itching for a fine home and fine clothes?' her father smiled.

'I can't help thinking that with your ability we ought to have them, yes. Possibly Ted Jackson's let me down because we don't amount to much.'

'Then if that's his angle he's better left alone. Now, about the money I need. I must find it somewhere. Any ideas?'

'None.' Margaret pulled up her chair to the table. 'People willing to give you thousands for a scientific invention only exist in fairy tales. Certainly I have no friends who'd spring it.'

'Then I must see a moneylender,' Jonas Glebe decided, coming over to settle at his supper. 'Once I've shown a model to the right party I'll not only collect my outlay and the interest, but thousands upon thousands on top of that! This, my dear, is really going to make us wealthy.'

Margaret did not appear very convinced. She had heard that promise before concerning 'gadgets' that had never made beyond a few pounds.

'Dad,' she said seriously, gripping his hand across the table, 'why can't you come down to earth for a moment? If you have a marvellous bomb there, all you have to do is submit the sketch to the War Office and have their experts look it over. They won't steal it. If it's worth anything you'll get all the money you need for research.'

'No.' Her father shook his head. 'I'm not at all convinced that the War Office would be interested. This bomb of mine has other uses besides warfare. It can be invaluable in mining, demolition, and similar projects. It could even be timed for use as a fog-signal! In any case I've already made up my mind who I'll contact.'

'Well?'

'Miles Rutter. He's one of our biggest industrial men and controls all manner of corporations and organisations. If I can sell to him I'll make all the money I need.'

Margaret sighed. 'Very well: but I do wish you'd not talk so glibly about going to a money-lender. Heaven knows where we'll end if you do.'

'We'll come out on top,' her father smiled, obsessed — as he usually was at the climax of an inventive session — with complete optimism. 'I'll fix things in the morning.'

Apparently he did, too, for when Margaret arrived home the following evening she found the small living room had been converted into something resembling a workshop. Apparatus lay in all directions and the table was littered with pieces of metal, springs, wires, and a collection of obviously new tools. Her father was busy at the bureau, using it now as a not too satisfactory bench. From the gleam in his tired eyes he appeared supremely happy.

'Hello, dear!' He barely glanced up. 'Fix the tea, will you? I haven't had time.'

Margaret went to work as instructed, asking a question meanwhile. 'You got the money, then?'

'Yes — from a moneylender. I traded in some insurance policies as security. None of which matters to me. This model must be completed — and it will take me about a month to do it. I should have an excellent chance of selling just at present with the international situation being so unsettled — '

2

Murder

On a cold, windy morning in mid-March Jonas Glebe could have been seen walking along a corridor of imitation marble and gleaming chrome, carrying a small suit-case in his hand.

Presently, in the midst of the opulent wilderness, he caught sight of a trim, uniformed girl hurrying into the distance with a message on a tray. He called somewhat timidly.

'Oh, miss! Have you a moment?'

She came over to him, pleasantly smiling. 'Can I help you, sir?'

'Yes young lady, you certainly can! I never thought the Rutter edifice was such a big, confusing place. I'd like to see Mister Rutter, if possible. It's extremely urgent.'

'Have you an appointment?'

'I'm afraid not, but surely you can help

me? I'm Jonas Glebe, a scientist. It is most essential I see Mister Rutter and nobody else. There just isn't time to make an appointment.'

The girl looked as though she wondered how this could be possible; then noticing Jonas Glebe's obvious weariness she seemed to make up her mind.

'I'll do what I can, sir. A scientific matter, you say?'

'Yes, yes. It's concerned with — with a bomb. I have it here.'

The girl stared in horror at the suitcase, and then hastily excused herself. When she returned she was minus tray and looking apprehensive. Keeping her distance she said:

'If you will come this way, Mister Glebe? Mister Rutter will see you.'

Jonas Glebe got up from the seat into which he had sunk exhausted. 'Thank you, thank you. I am so much obliged — Oh, you needn't be afraid,' he added, smiling, as the girl still kept several feet away. 'When I said a bomb I meant a model one, without explosive. I'd hardly be so foolish as to walk through the streets of London with a live bomb in my suitcase.'

'You'd be surprised, sir, if you knew the cranks we do get here sometimes,' the girl said, leading the way into a lift, and in a few moments Jonas Glebe found himself whirled to the top-floor of the edifice.

Here the girl led him along a thickly-carpeted corridor to a black door marked PRIVATE and there left him, once again with almost indecent haste. Glebe smiled to himself and knocked on the portal in front of him.

'Come in, come in!' boomed a voice from beyond, so Glebe entered, closing the door behind him.

For a moment or two he stood blinking at an office of extraordinary size. He felt — and looked — insignificant amidst the hide chairs, the walnut desks and cabinets. Then from the biggest desk in the array the voice boomed again.

'Hello there, Mister Glebe! Do come in!' The voice was powerful, even friendly, yet somehow it sounded artificial.

Glebe moved onwards to the main desk and grasped the fleshy paw held out to him. For a second or so he stood studying the man who nearly everybody knew, and of whom not a few were afraid. Miles Rutter was the grey-headed, immaculately dressed master of the Rutter Investment Trust, which did not limit itself to this huge building, either.

'Sit down, Mister Glebe — you look tired. Have a cigar — ' Rutter pushed over a silver box with a hand flashing gems.

'No, no, thank you, Mister Rutter. I don't smoke much, and when I do it is only a pipe.' Glebe sat down heavily and continued his survey of the man to whom he hoped to sell his 'wares'. He was not deceived by the effusiveness. Miles Rutter was no philanthropist. His cold grey eyes and rattrap mouth were proof enough of that. These, added to an intelligent forehead, contrived to portray a man of untiring energy and tremendous ambition.

For his own part Miles Rutter had already decided that his visitor was a fool, like the rest of the crackpot scientists who took up his time, but there was always the chance that one of them might have something, so he never turned them down.

'From the clerk who announced you I learn you referred to a bomb,' Rutter said, inspecting the end of his cigar.

Glebe gave a little start. 'Er — yes. Forgive me, I was daydreaming. Yes, a new type of bomb. So far I haven't tried to interest anybody in it. I came straight to you.'

'Did you now?' Rutter grinned broadly revealing strong natural teeth. 'Why? Do I look like Santa Claus?'

'No. I just felt a sort of — *urge* that way. It's hard to explain.'

'I see. Well, what about this bomb? Not that I'm connected with the War Office, remember!'

'I know, but you have big armament concerns. I've checked upon that. You see, my fear is that if I offer this bomb of mine to the War Office they'll say it's too barbaric, too horrifying and insidious to use.'

'And you believe I won't have any such qualms?'

'I believe exactly that.'

Rutter chuckled. 'You may be right. I am not a man of emotions, Mister Glebe.'

'That is why, in my belief that you can make use of this invention of mine, I have come to you. I am desperately in need of money. My daughter and I have very little. I thought that perhaps — '

'Perhaps — yes, yes. You'll not find me hard to deal with, my dear sir. However, we can do nothing until you explain, or demonstrate. So how about it?'

'I can demonstrate at this very moment if you wish.'

'Splendid! Come this way.'

Rutter got to his feet — he was quite a short man when standing — and strode like a prize bullock to a doorway, opened it and ushered Glebe beyond it. A white-clad technician with sharp blue eyes and fluffy brown hair came forward expectantly.

'Mister Glebe, I'd like you to meet my scientific advisor, Doctor Standish. Standish, my dear fellow — here is a bomb. Mister Glebe, I rely implicitly on his judgment. He has, by his opinions, made or broken more men than I can remember.'

Standish shook hands and smiled without emotion, then evidently thinking he should explain Rutter's statement he said: 'I see some hundred of so-called scientific inventions in a month, very few of which are of any use. Fortunately there is a disturbed international horizon at the moment so a new type of bomb might be worth consideration.'

'So I'm hoping,' Glebe responded, fiddling with the catches on his suitcase. 'You see, my bomb sinks through the ground as a stone sinks through water. It will explode where you want and when you want. Rather devastating, don't you think?'

Rutter and Standish glanced sharply at each other without Glebe even noticing; he was still busy on the obstinate catches of his suitcase.

'Interesting, anyway,' Rutter responded guardedly, and drew at his cigar.

'Sounds impossible to me,' Standish commented, and Rutter gave a chuckle as Glebe glanced up.

'Take no notice of him, Mister Glebe! He's become soured by so many disappointments. Just you get busy and show us what you can do. The place is yours.'

Rutter sat down, crossed his fat legs, and still pulled steadily at his cigar. Standish waited, one eyebrow raised in doubt as with the methodical care of a man accustomed to handling dangerous articles Glebe extracted a small metal ball from the suitcase. He looked around him for a moment, the ball in his hand, and finally decided upon an empty metal table supported on a single central pillar bolted firmly to the floor.

'Is that pillar solid or hollow?' Glebe asked.

'Solid,' Standish pronounced, and folded his arms.

'Thank you. Now, watch carefully, please. This may spoil your table, but it is worth it for the sake of demonstration. Nothing else appears so convenient.'

Glebe pulled a small pin out of the metal ball that he opened, then taking from his waistcoat pocket a screw of cotton wool, he extracted a little black pill and fed it to the bomb. 'Just two grains of *Glebenite* — an explosive of my own invention, gentlemen,' he explained calmly, as he gently placed the now closed ball on the tabletop, making sure it did not roll. Almost immediately the sphere glowed slightly and began to sink quickly out of sight. The hole it made in the process closed up again with a slight sucking of air and the tabletop was smooth once more. Three minutes or so passed and then came a dull report. The pillar of the table exploded with moderate violence, toppling the structure to the floor.

Instantly Rutter sprang to his feet, staring. Standish blinked once. Glebe only smiled and considered the wreckage.

'Just what did you do?' Standish asked at last, incredulous.

'The model bomb sank through the solid metal and exploded at the predetermined point at the base of the pillar,' Glebe explained. 'Had I wished, I could have made it sink right through this building to the foundations.'

'A — a self-sinking bomb!' Rutter

exclaimed, striding forward.

'Exactly. I call it the G-Bomb. 'G' for Glebe and 'G' for gravity, which is its main factor, of course. It can be made to sink to any required depth by an adjustment of the mechanism. All perfectly simple yet, unhappily, somewhat diabolical.'

Rutter took a deep breath and gave another sharp glance at his scientific advisor. Standish gave a quiet nod, but he looked puzzled. Had he not known the table pillar was solid steel he would have put the demonstration down to a clever conjuring trick.

'Just how do you explain it, Mister Glebe?' he asked.

'It's all perfectly simple,' Glebe responded, shrugging, 'So much so that I wonder scientists have not happened on it long before this. I'll outline it to you with pleasure, but you must forgive me if I retain the exact details in regard to mechanisms and so forth until we come to terms — if we come to terms!'

'Oh, come now, I'm sure there will be no trouble about that!' Rutter exclaimed grandiloquently, putting a thick fatherly arm about Glebe's thin shoulders. 'By all means retain the details: I'd consider you a fool if you didn't. Just tell us in simple terms what the secret is.'

'Well first of all, anything must move downwards towards the Earth's centre because of the law of gravitation. This particular idea began one day when my thoughts unexpectedly pictured a stone sinking into a bog. Don't ask me what started that train of thought — '

'We won't,' Rutter assured quickly. 'Please continue.'

'Suppose, I asked myself, suppose something could be invented to sink through *solids*? Suppose a form of explosive able to blow up at any depth without previous drilling? It seemed to me that this might be immensely useful in laying foundations, opening up mines, and so forth — '

'Yes, yes,' Standish interrupted impatiently, 'but the explanation?'

'Ah, yes. Well, I devised a small mechanism,' Glebe opened the hemispheres of an unused bomb from his suitcase and pointed to the intricate internal workings. 'You, Doctor Standish, may follow the idea. Solids are composed of atoms and atoms are constructed like miniature solar systems. In other words, if you picture them from a sideways angle, they are flat, but this flatness points in all directions. It is not organised. Because of this no solid can fall through another: no two solids can occupy the same space at the same time. Atoms have poles, but they point in all directions. I found that by magnetism I could make them point — every single one of them — in one direction. There are magnets in this bomb, as you can see — '

Standish reflected for a moment and then he said: 'In which case you would make the atoms all flat — parallel — so that they would only block about fifteen per cent of the space they occupied in the disordered form?'

'That's it,' Glebe acknowledged, with his weary little smile. 'That slight resistance causes my bomb to sink slowly and not immediately. The force of gravity, which of course operates under all

41

conditions, draws the bomb downward and the bomb's magnetism straightens the atomic formations on the journey. Hence, nothing can stop it: it just sinks. In short, it is a case of passing one solid through another, and the moment the bomb has passed and the magnetism has gone the atoms disorder again leaving the former solidity and no trace of what has happened. That is why there is no bore left in the table stand where the bomb travelled; the steel atoms reformed to cover all traces of its passage.'

'Amazing!' Rutter whispered, half to himself. 'Positively amazing!' He seemed inordinately fascinated by the idea; then suddenly making up his mind he caught Glebe by the arm. 'Come into my office, Mister Glebe. There are details to be arranged. Financial details,' he purred, now as friendly as a tiger which has gorged itself.

Glebe nodded and picked up his case. Methodically he put the unused bomb into it and then snapped over the catches. After a struggle they held firm.

'I need a new one,' he explained

sheepishly. 'Perhaps, if you like my invention, I might even — '

'Like it!' Rutter cried. 'Why, man alive, it's colossal! Come along — ' He led the way into the office. 'Sit down, do. Now — ' Rutter flopped at his desk, breathed hard, and then pressed a button. 'In a case like this you can name your own figure, Mister Glebe — within reason, of course.'

'I — I thought perhaps — ten million for the exclusive rights in the bomb.' Glebe looked half scared at the suggestion, but Rutter did not even hesitate.

'Ten million it shall be! And you shall have your cheque before you leave this office — ' Rutter looked up as Valentine Turner, his young personal secretary, came into the office. He looked more like a champion wrestler than a secretary — blond-headed, massive-shouldered, hazel-eyed. There had been moments when his secretarial work had been merged into that of bodyguard.

'Turner, make out a contract and a cheque for ten million pounds,' Rutter ordered. 'Usual phraseology — all rights.

Quick as you can and I'll sign both.'

'Yes, sir.' Val Turner glanced at the scientist and then went back into his own adjoining office.

'I suppose,' Rutter asked, when the door had closed, 'that you have got this G-Bomb patented? The patent rights automatically become mine by reason of the contract.'

'Patent!' Glebe gave a start. 'Why of course! I knew I was going to do something: my daughter reminded me — Well, it doesn't really signify now, does it?'

'Not a bit,' Rutter replied cordially. 'In fact it makes things easier — much easier.'

Glebe began to fumble once more with his suitcase, finally opened it, and said: 'I have here all the details, the scientific prints, samples of the magnetic bars — everything. You can soon work out the details.'

'Take them over, Standish,' Rutter instructed, as the scientist came in from the adjoining laboratory.

'You can probably see why the thing is

basically so diabolical?' Glebe asked anxiously. 'Imagine such a bomb in warfare! It could be dropped anywhere and leave no trace until it blew up. Naturally, I didn't invent the bomb for that purpose, but in a crisis — '

Val Turner came back with papers and cheque in hand. In a moment Rutter had appended his signature to both and then sat watching Glebe's thin hand clutching the pen.

'It is not often I meet a real scientist, Mister Glebe,' he said finally handing over the cheque. 'Drop in whenever you wish. Turner, see Mister Glebe safely out of the building.'

Glebe gathered up his hat and empty case. 'Thank you Mister Rutter — over again. You don't know what this money will mean to Margaret and me. We've been so restricted and — '

'Of course, of course.' Rutter smiled at the scientist and secretary from the office, watching the door close. When he turned again his smile had gone and his mouth was a hard line across his face.

'Well, Standish? It's genuine, of course?'

'The real thing! The simplest and yet the most brilliant invention of its kind I've ever seen. It was worth all of that ten million pounds, believe me.'

'Believe it or not,' Rutter said, 'that old fool forgot to patent his invention!'

'No record, then, of his ever having invented it?'

'That's the situation.' Rutter gazed thoughtfully at the plans and material Glebe had left behind. 'This is manna from heaven!' he exclaimed, rubbing his bejewelled hands. 'Think of it! Bombs that leave no trace! At last we have the ideal means of consummating our campaign: we can tear this or any other country wide open! We have the agents, the rings, the societies, all ready to go to work the moment I give the order. Up to now we have been held up by lack of something effective, and now it is put right into our hands. Yes! We can sow the country with these invisible dealers of death. Thousands of them, manufactured in my own industrial works, and with the infinite money supply of the Cause. We have waited and hoped for a day like this,

Standish, and at last it is here!'

'I'm afraid I don't concern myself with ideologies, Mister Rutter,' Standish replied, shrugging. 'I'm a scientist and prepared to work for the Cause: but as a man I rather deplore the inhuman cunning of this invention. Baffles me how a man of Glebe's obvious simplicity could ever have conceived it.'

'He said something about watching — or thinking about — a stone sinking in a bog. Curious how irrelevances can lead the mind on.'

'Very.'

Rutter smiled — but it was his eyes at which Standish gazed. Their greyness was icy and didn't match his lips. Standish had seen that danger signal oft-times before. Without a word he picked up the plans and the model.

'Better see what we've got for our millions,' he said, and left the office.

It was close on seven in the evening and most of the Trust staff had left for home when Standish came out of his laboratory again, smiling in satisfaction.

'Have you a moment, Mister Rutter?'

he asked, advancing to the desk where Rutter was still working on a stack of papers.

'If it's important, yes. If not, no.'

'I've examined the G-Bomb.'

'Well what about it?' Rutter sat back in his chair and lighted a fresh cigar.

'Just this. We can make bombs of any size and use any kind of explosive we wish. Adjustment of the mechanism times the instant of explosion and the duration of the magnetism. That means we could send the thing down five feet or five miles. No limit until we get to the centre of the Earth. There have been plenty of deadly weapons in history, but none the equal of this. I want your orders. All we need now is to manufacture, so what do I do?'

Rutter considered for a while, then he said: 'We might as well use all our own key factories in north, south, east and west. Consolidated Steel can handle it. The Rutter Trust is Consolidated Steel, so we've nothing there to worry about. You know more than I do about explosives and such-like; so work out a campaign.

Pass the information on through the usual channels so the network can start to operate. I'll give you further instructions later.'

The scientist nodded, then he and Rutter both looked up as the outer door opened to admit two impassive individuals in soft hats and overcoats. The taller one tossed an oblong slip of paper on the desk.

'Ten million pounds, chief,' he announced briefly.

Rutter frowned, and then he grinned. He picked up the cheque and slowly tore it in pieces.

'You mean — Jonas Glebe?' Standish asked levelly.

'Naturally.' Rutter eyed the strong-arm man. 'What happened to our doddering friend?'

'He was run over,' the man answered, sighing. 'Naturally we rushed to help him — and I took the cheque from him in the process. We were too late. Hit and run driver got him and then made off so fast we didn't even get his number.'

'More plainly, he was murdered!' Standish snapped.

'A hit and run driver, Standish,' Rutter murmured soothingly. 'Didn't you hear what Joe said? If they find the driver I'll put the clamps down and stop things being traced back to here. If they don't — Well, I'm afraid Mister Glebe was a fool to let his invention go without a patent. Nobody can ever prove he owned it.'

' 'Cept his daughter,' Joe announced sourly.

'Of course, the daughter! I'd forgotten her. What about her?'

'I dunno, chief. I haven't seen her — '

'Then find her, you idiot!' Rutter shouted. 'I want the whole Glebe family tree chopped down. Not a trace must be left! Too dangerous. Do what you like, but get her. I'll see you're protected.'

The strong-arm men went out and Standish watched them go, his lips tight.

'I'm not altogether sure I like this indiscriminate elimination, Mister Rutter,' he remarked.

'No? You worry about things scientific, doctor, and leave the rest to me.'

'What if we get across the authorities?

It won't be just us who'll be damaged: it will smash the entire Cause in pieces — '

'Oh, shut up!' Rutter snorted. 'We're not going to get across with anybody: everything's too well organised for that. Stop bleating and — '

He paused in surprise as a ray of light flooded from the wall opposite. Val Turner came quietly out of his secretarial office, his hat and coat on. He switched off the light in his sanctum and closed the door.

'What the hell do you want?' Rutter blazed at him.

'I, sir?' Turner returned a level stare. 'Nothing. Except to tell you that I have finished my reports. They're on my desk. Will that be all for tonight?'

Rutter sat gazing into the young man's unflinching eyes for a moment and then he slowly nodded.

'Yes. That will be all for tonight.'

'Goodnight, sir. 'Night, Doctor Standish.'

Turner went out quietly and then Rutter's eyes flashed up to the open ventilator above Turner's office door. Standish followed his master's gaze, and gave a start.

'Great heavens, Mr. Rutter, you don't suppose he heard about the — '

'Possibly. I thought he'd gone home. If his door had had glass in it we'd have seen the light shining.' Rutter gave a grim look. 'Let him start trying to prove something and I'll smack him down so hard he'll stay put for the rest of his life. Now, Standish, I've some work to finish.'

Meantime Val Turner was walking through the quiet expanses of the Trust Building with grim thoughts in his mind. He had heard every word of Rutter's through the office ventilator, albeit unintentionally.

'Seems to me it confirms all Rita said,' he muttered, letting himself down from the heights in the personal elevator. Rita was his wife. 'Said he was a crook deep down, and I wouldn't believe her. He's a murderer, hundred percent, and I just couldn't see it. I must have been crazy!'

He left the elevator and nodded goodnight to the watchman, then he went out into the brightly-lit street. It was only a short distance to his flat. Lost in thought he marched along, until when he was halfway along a dark side street something prodded him in the back.

'Keep going, and don't turn around.'

He was surprised to note that the voice was a woman's, low and vindictive.

'Might I ask what the idea is?' he questioned, still continuing walking.

'Just let me do the talking, will you? I'm Margaret Glebe, daughter of Jonas Glebe, the inventor of the G-Bomb. Does that mean anything to you?'

Val Turner remained silent, frowning to himself. The girl's grim voice went on:

'Just three hours ago I had arranged to meet my father, and I saw him run down! Brutally slain! I was only across the road when it happened. We'd promised to meet at the Grecian Café after his interview with Rutter. The 'accident' looked like the work of a hit and run driver, but it wasn't. It was planned — planned by that low-down barbarian Miles Rutter. I've heard a good deal about him but shut my mind to it: now I wish I had warned dad to keep clear of him.'

'Whilst my sympathies are entirely with you, Miss Glebe, I must point out that I had nothing to do with it. Why pick on me particularly?'

'You're connected with Rutter, otherwise you wouldn't be leaving the Trust Building at this hour in the evening. You are all I need. Two other men left just before you but I just couldn't tackle them: they were too powerful. So I waited hoping to get Rutter himself. Instead you came out, quite easy to handle — '

'What makes you think so?'

Val Turner twirled round abruptly, fully expecting the savage blaze of a revolver in his ribs, but instead his action knocked a small hand-torch into the gutter. The girl looked down at it and then faced him. He could see her face was white and trembling with both grief and anger.

'That — was the gun?' Turner asked, picking up the torch.

'Yes,' she whispered, as he gave it back to her. 'I just don't know what I'm doing! Honest I don't!' I'm worried sick! She put the torch in her rainproof and then sighed. 'Well, there it is. Hand me over for assault and have done with it. You're entitled to.'

'I think you've got me all wrong, Miss Glebe,' Val said seriously. 'It so happens that I know your father was murdered, but I had nothing to do with it. It was Rutter's doing, his entirely. You say you saw your father run down. I assume you let the police on the spot know your identity?'

'No.'

'What! But why on earth — '

'I didn't tell anybody. I think I went crazy.' The girl's voice was coming in jerks. 'I just thought up this idiotic plan to catch somebody belonging to Rutter's organisation and make him confess the truth to the police. If only you knew what this all means!' she cried hoarsely. 'This bomb my father invented is a terrible weapon. He said so himself, and in the wrong hands — '

'That it's in the wrong hands seems to me beyond doubt,' Turner interrupted. 'Your father sold it to Rutter for ten million pounds. I made out the contract myself — but Rutter took the cheque back by force after the 'accident' to your father. Apparently he had no patent right on the invention, therefore there's no evidence that he invented the bomb.'

'But he did! I swear he did! So after all he forgot to patent it! I might have known it.'

'I know he invented the bomb, Miss Glebe, and so do you, but you and I are the only two people who can prove that Rutter stole and murdered — '

'Don't be too sure of that, Turner!'

Turner and the girl turned together. The figures of two men in soft hats and big overcoats were dimly visible in the shadow of a nearby doorway. Without warning a gun blazed suddenly. Margaret Glebe's lips parted in a half-cry, then with both hands at her left breast she toppled forward and crashed motionless on the pavement.

'Work that one out, Mister Turner,' came a sneering voice, and the still smoking gun was flipped towards him from the gloom to clatter at his feet.

Before Turner had a chance to collect his wits, doors and windows seemed to sprout open all around him from the high tenement houses. Men and women appeared, drawn by the noise of the firing. They stared at the bewildered Turner, at the gun, and the sprawled young woman.

Utterly confused by the rapidity of everything Turner heard pronouncements from the general jabbering of voices.

'This woman is dead — shot through the heart!'

'Come on, you!' Turner found himself seized. Grim-jawed officers seemed to be all around him —

★　★　★

Miles Rutter was just leaving his office for the night when the private wire buzzed.

'Well?' he asked briefly, and it was the voice of strong-arm Joe that replied.

'We got on the track of the Glebe girl as you told us, chief. Spotted her not far from the Trust Building. At least we reckoned it was her from the way she was behaving. We followed her, and in case you don't know it Turner knows all about the killing of old man Glebe. He told the daughter that much.'

'Then why the devil didn't you — '

'We did, chief. We shot the girl through the heart and left Turner to explain it. It's up to you now. You can stick a murder charge on him if you want. I'll be at Toni's Café if I'm needed.'

Rutter smiled. 'Remind me to give you a bonus, Joe. Goodnight.'

3

Rutter strikes

The machinations of Miles Rutter thereafter were far-reaching. Val Turner, for reasons best known to himself, refused to say anything in his own defence. His lawyer talked himself hoarse, using what little evidence he could find. Most of it had been supplied by Val Turner's wife — and the extraordinary thing was that Rita Turner was partially successful in her fight against the Colossus. At least she dug up enough to make portions of the charge against her husband seem doubtful. Notwithstanding, he still received a life sentence.

It seemed to him that his world had crashed in ruins. He remembered his wife's brave, tear-stained face in the courtroom; then he found it replaced by the inflexible visages of the warders. Prison, grey and inexorable, filled the future.

To Rutter the verdict caused some irritation and he was not slow to say as much.

'Turner is out of the way behind prison walls, yes, where he can't prove anything,' he said bitterly, 'but he isn't dead! As long as he lives there is always the slender chance that he might escape, and if he should — '

'He'll leave nothing unturned to give you what you deserve, eh?' Standish suggested dryly.

'He'll be vindictive!' Rutter corrected, glaring. 'His wife is no fool, either. She almost got up enough evidence to get the life penalty quashed, and I have the uneasy feeling that she hasn't finished yet. I don't like it.'

Standish could somehow feel what was developing. 'If you are planning to wipe her out too, Mister Rutter, count me out! That killing of Margaret Glebe was too close to the hairline for my liking. Next time you may not be so lucky. I value my neck even if you don't.'

Rutter's next words seemed to indicate that he had dropped the subject. 'What about those bombs, Standish? How much longer will you be?'

'I'm ready now. I followed out your orders and got several thousand bombs manufactured. They're being distributed through the usual undercover channels to our agents.'

'And the aircraft factories? We're ready there?'

'Completely. When you give the word the underground factories will be ready to disgorge. Our agents, by the use of the G-Bombs, can sabotage every defence point — including missile bases — in Britain. We can have the whole country under our heel at any time we want. Our air armada, when released, will crush all opposition by terror-bombing alone.'

'Mmmm.' Rutter pondered. 'How far down do you plan to sink the G-Bombs under industrial and defence centres?'

'About a quarter of a mile. That ought to be sufficient.'

'I don't think so! I don't just want an ordinary explosion to wreck vital centres: I want the entire centres to drop down a mine from which they can never be retrieved — '

'It can't be done, Mister Rutter.' Standish shook his head deliberately. 'We have to remember that Earth has inner forces. If we drop the bombs too deep they might split a volcanic seam, then anything could happen.'

'As long as we have the Cause ruling the country at the finish of the campaign I don't care if we release hell itself!' Rutter retorted. 'Sink those bombs down five miles. When they blow up I want mines into which men and units and buildings will drop, understand?'

'It's too big a risk!' Standish protested. 'I'm a scientist and I beg of you to listen to me — '

'I'm not going to argue, Standish. I have instructed our European headquarters to sink their bombs five miles down and we'll do the same here.'

Standish's face was suddenly grey with worry. He had a mental picture of agents of the Cause scattered in their sneaking thousands about the Earth dropping the silent, self sinking bombs in all manner of places. He was a scientist; Rutter was not. Therein lay tragedy.

'Finished?' Rutter asked coldly.

Standish made an effort. 'Sorry. I was just thinking that if one of those bombs rips a volcanic seam it might easily blow the lid off a whole continent! We're fighting for the Cause and the ultimate domination of the world, not the total destruction of everything it contains. You've got to stop at a quarter-mile depth for safety's sake. Explosions are okay, but wholesale subsidences are another thing altogether.' Rutter smiled, but Standish was looking at the eyes. 'I know what I'm talking about, Mister Rutter,' Standish insisted, not very vehemently.

'Yes, of course you do,' Rutter purred. 'Of course, I'll do just as you say — Now get out!' he yelled. 'The Cause has no use for men who are afraid to take chances. *Get out!*'

Standish left, perspiration dewing his face. The eyes of Rutter seemed to be in the corridor before him. Too many times had Rutter smiled only with his lips —

⋆　⋆　⋆

The evening papers carried a column headed:

RUTTER TRUST SCIENTIST FOUND DROWNED

Nobody attempted to offer an explanation, beyond suicide. For that matter nobody could — except Rita Turner. Stanley Wade of the Special Investigation Branch of Scotland Yard was surprised when Rita was shown into his office. In a moment he knew from her sombre dark eyes and taut mouth that something was wrong. He greeted her pleasantly enough and drew up a chair for her. She was not by any means a stranger. Ever since Val Turner had been sent to the penitentiary Rita had tried to make Wade interest himself in finding damning proof against Miles Rutter — without success.

'You heard of the death of Doctor Standish, the scientist of the Rutter Trust?' Rita enquired, as Wade settled at his desk once more.

'Yes I heard. You mean his suicide?'

'It wasn't suicide, Inspector. It was

deliberate, cold-blooded murder. Standish was slain just as were Mister Glebe and his daughter Margaret. I've said all along, and still say, that my husband was wrongfully convicted.'

'I can only repeat what I have said before, Mrs. Turner — that the rights and wrongs of that business were decided by judge and jury. There's nothing I can do about that.'

'I'm not asking you to any more because I believe Val is safer in jail than out of it. What I am suggesting is that you and the authorities generally open their eyes a bit! Three deaths in succession — three! — and all of them connected with the Rutter Trust. The facts at my husband's trial showed some totally false love affair to be the cause of him shooting Margaret Glebe. Corruption and wrangling in legal circles, backed by Rutter, and my husband's own silence, stopped the truth from getting out. Margaret Glebe was murdered, Inspector, by Rutter's strong-arm men, just as her father was murdered by a hit-and-run driver in Rutter's employ. Rutter destroyed Glebe for one good reason. He feared his scientific knowledge — and another reason was that Rutter didn't want ten million pounds to go out of his bank.'

Wade leaned forward a little. 'You've said a good deal more on this occasion than ever before, Mrs. Turner. May I ask from where you have accumulated all this information concerning Rutter?'

'Val himself told me. I saw him in jail on visitor's day. He told me all these facts.'

'Why on earth didn't he give them at the trial?'

'Oh can't you see?' Rita asked hopelessly. 'He just didn't dare! To have gained his liberty by indicting Rutter would have made him a certain target for killers all over the city — killers under Rutter's control. Anyway, Rutter would have wriggled free and Val's life would have been jeopardised from that moment onwards. He preferred to gain the protection of jail and afterwards work from comparative safety — through me — to prove his innocence.'

'You see, Val was Rutter's personal secretary — as you will remember from the facts at the trial — and he made out the contract and cheque for ten million pounds to Glebe. The contract was for a new type of bomb, which fact hasn't been mentioned up to now. A bomb that can sink itself through the ground or any solid. In the present state of international tension isn't that more than significant?'

'Sinks through the ground or any solid?' Wade repeated musing. 'I don't quite understand.'

Rita gave a troubled smile. 'I am afraid, Inspector that you, like the rest of the authorities, think that Miles Rutter is limited to a Financial House in the city. That isn't so, as Val well knows. A whole network of steelworks and industries are controlled by Rutter, and they in turn are cover-ups for more sinister activities. The things Rutter is doing are dangerous in the extreme. They menace every man and woman in the land, and maybe the world. I insist that you investigate him and all his activities! Do it in the interest of general safety, not particularly to clear Val. That will follow logically, and he is safe enough at the present.'

Wade sat thinking for a while, then finally he said: 'It all sounds very fantastic to me, Mrs. Turner, and I can't help but think that if anything really important were going on beneath the surface, our Intelligence Department would know all about it. The War Department too.'

'Even if Rutter agents happened to be in both departments?'

'Oh come now, Mrs. Turner, you're not suggesting — '

'I certainly am!' Rita snapped. 'Miles Rutter is an organising genius, an utterly ruthless man with tremendous ambition. By birth he is not British, I've checked up on it. All this is the honest truth, Inspector. It can't hurt you to check on it, anyway.'

'Very well,' Wade promised. 'I'll do what I can. Now you've given me all this fresh information I have something to work on.'

'In the meantime,' Rita finished, 'I want protective custody. Now I've told you all this I'm not risking going alone into the outer world again. I know what I'm up against, and so will you before long!'

Ten days later, Miles Rutter got first wind of what was coming. It happened when Angorstine, his ablest agent, cesspool for orders and instructions of strictest secrecy between the European connections and the big man himself, learned of the thing he had feared for a long time. Immediately he headed for Rutter's city office, deserting the complex post he filled somewhere in a European Embassy.

'What's the idea of risking coming here?' Rutter demanded in anger. 'You know it's dangerous!'

The square-headed, thick-lipped Angorstine had a ready answer, and he delivered it in his unemotional voice: 'Dangerous, sir, yes, but I thought it better to take the risk and come personally than use a telephone. Scotland Yard's out to clean up our entire organisation.'

'I've known that for years. What's the matter with you, man? Nerves?'

'This is the real thing. Every man is working on it, and it smells like dynamite.'

Rutter stared amazedly. 'But they don't

know a thing — '

'Yes they do. I've been told that Turner, your ex-secretary, told his wife a good deal on her visit to the prison. She told Wade at the Yard and apparently convinced him. Now the machinery is moving a sight too rapidly and surely for comfort!'

Rutter slammed his fist on the desk. 'I'll get that Turner woman if it's the last thing I do. I knew it wasn't safe letting Turner go on living. I'll see his wife is — '

'You can't, sir. She asked for — and got — protective custody.'

Rutter's lips twitched at news of the setback. Angorstine went on talking with renewed urgency. 'Either we act now or never, Mister Rutter. If once we are discovered our whole campaign will be wiped out before we can do a thing, but if we strike we can carry all before us. Doctor Standish left everything ready. Our agents are everywhere, ready to set those G-Bombs going down five miles, just as you ordered. All key points are covered. In other parts of the world everything is ready too. The Cause can blast any and all the countries wide open. The war we launch can end in a few months — even weeks — and we shall be victorious.'

'It's forcing my hand,' Rutter said, gazing at the man's square, brutal face.

'If the authorities act faster than you do we're finished! Act! Give me the word and in three days we'll be well away. Give me an appointed time for the 'planes to move, the bombs to explode, for the defence units to be immobilised. Too late Britain will learn that she is being destroyed. The G-Bomb will bring the whole country smashing into the dust.'

Rutter set his mouth abruptly. 'Very well, Angorstine, get busy! Time the bombs for explosion six hours after sinking below ground surface. Time the entire movement forces for midnight, three days hence. I'll move to the underground headquarters. That's all.'

Angorstine went, smiling delightedly to himself.

Meanwhile, Stanley Wade was commencing to get the reports of his men operating the dragnet across Britain, and he was beginning to discover things that completely backed Rita Turner's vehement assertions. It seemed quite incredible!

'Agents of European power everywhere,' Wade breathed, looking through the papers on his desk. 'The country's infested with 'em! Spies! Spies to some mystical cause which believes — like many before it — that it can dominate the world.'

He looked up at the worried faces of the men of his department, all of them connected in some branch or other with public security.

'We have ourselves to blame, gentlemen,' Wade added. 'It is as Mrs. Turner said: we have taken far too much for granted in regard to Rutter. We allowed him to continue his activity, unsuspecting of his real influence in diverse places. We never realised then that the Consolidated Steel Corporation, the Blue Oil Combine, the International Federation and who knows how many other big enterprises, were connected with and, at root, controlled by him. His devilish tentacles are spread half over the world.'

'What do we do now then?' one of the men asked.

'Do? We have got to round up all these agents and the things they control. In the meantime I'll refer the matter to the Government. It's too international for the police alone to handle, and the danger is too great. I've got to have a parole for Turner, too. He knows plenty and can probably help us. The rest of you go to work as you see fit, and don't report without results.'

Thereafter wires began to buzz. Yard experts took fast 'planes in various directions. The whole law machine of Britain went to work in grim earnest, in collusion with the authorities of other countries, chiefly of Europe. In spite of an elastic censorship clamping the Press some of the news seeped through to a puzzled public.

The *Clarion* wanted to know: IS WAR IMMINENT? But it could not definitely answer its own question because of lack of facts, and since radio and television were also ordered to use hush-hush tactics there was no information forthcoming from this source either.

Miles Rutter, by now fully alive to the situation, worked unceasingly. Hour by hour there came through the multiple strands of his web a series of reports collected by Angorstine. Vital centres were already in hand. Bombs, accurately timed, were ready for midnight and in the desired positions, along every coast, in every public utility, in armament works, depots and Government offices. Throughout the length and breadth of the British Isles the undercover agents were at work.

On the third day the hours, fateful indeed for still puzzled Englishmen, crept onward, and the shadow deepened over peace. Inevitably news leaked out. There were hints of a lightning war with Europe, invasion by long-distance bombers, submarine attack — in fact probably everything was thought of except destruction from within.

Certainly nobody except Val Turner thought of self-sinking bombs! His parole had been granted by an extraordinary Board Meeting, and he thought of the G-Bombs as he sat in the Government 'plane whirling him quickly over the countryside, towards London.

'Pretty dark down there — not a glimmer of light,' he commented, and his guard gave a grim nod.

'Yes. Black-out's in force. Just a precaution. Seems to be something blowing up.'

'I suppose,' Val said, 'you don't know what Scotland Yard paroled me for?'

'Even if I did — which I don't — it wouldn't be up to me to say anything. I was ordered to collect and deliver. The rest is up to Inspector Wade. You'll find out everything when we reach London.'

Val became silent. He had pretty well guessed why he was wanted. He knew that nothing short of national necessity and his knowledge of Miles Rutter could have obtained parole for him so soon. He sat turning the matter over in his mind, gazing onto the darkness outside.

Even London itself was partially blacked-out. The public in general, baffled by the obviously serious turn in events and lack of news, seemed to be thronging the gloomy streets. The police car had to siren its way through seething crowds to Scotland Yard.

Inside the building Wade's office was brightly lighted. He looked tired and worried and had his jacket off to his task. In the office there were also officials and, in a far corner, Rita Turner herself. She sprang to her feet in joy as Val entered.

Wade allowed them their brief, earnest greeting and then he said curtly: 'Turner, it looks as though your story we heard through your wife here is only too true. Pity is we're late. I sent for you so you can give us more details. Granting there is time to act on them, that is.'

'Details? Gladly! How much do you want to know? Miles Rutter is an enemy agent, one of the biggest that ever was, of continental birth and obeying, remotely, continental masters. He's a — '

'Yes, yes, I know all about that. Do you know the names of any of his agents?'

Val shook his head. 'Afraid not, Inspector. Every man and woman working secretly for him had a number. I used to think that they were contract numbers until I got to musing over them in prison. Then it dawned on me that they must be agents.'

'How many?'

'Hard to remember, but I think the number went up to about ninety-two-thousand.'

Wade threw up his hands and looked around him.

'There we are, gentlemen! From these reports here I calculated about ninety-thousand men and women in the pay of a foreign power. Some of them — in fact most of them — are supposed to be good-living British citizens, or at any rate they seek shelter under our flag. They are employees of Rutter — his trusted workers. Saboteurs — spies — rats! For over two years Rutter has been at work planning for the total destruction of this country. Through a slip-up Turner here got a clue. In a few days we have tried to catch up on the greatest organised effort to destroy a country ever yet made. I don't see how we're to do it. We can't rope in ninety-thousand suspects in a few days — or even hours. I haven't any idea how much time we have left.'

'Get Rutter himself,' Turner suggested. 'He's the chief. The others will vanish if he does.'

'Knowing Rutter is guilty is one thing: proving it is another,' Wade retorted. 'He is fenced in by a wall of legal preventions which would require months of intensified effort to break down. We're working on it, never fear. We have collected some of the agents and pinned them down to confessions. We've got something, I say, but not by any means enough. That's where you come in, Turner. I want you to try and recall every detail of your employment with Rutter. You must — '

Wade swung round as the 'phone buzzed. His face assumed various expressions as he listened. He kept on nodding, then with a grunt of acknowledgement he put the instrument back on its cradle.

'Intelligence,' he explained. 'A report has just been received that two-hundred heavy bombing 'planes have been massed on an airfield near the Channel in Europe.'

'One of our airfields over there?' asked an Air Ministry man sharply.

'No — and that's the point,' Wade responded, thinking. 'This information I have just received has also been relayed to all defence points in England: they have all been alerted. Those 'planes do not belong to any known power. They're grey and unidentified. They may have been brought from some secret factory in Europe. Since there are nearly twenty Rutter organisations scattered around Europe under different names that is more than possible. If one factory can produce two-hundred 'planes the rest is simple arithmetic. Twenty factories — two-hundred 'planes each — four thousand 'planes, and not one of them ours.'

'You mean,' Turner asked slowly, 'that we're too late?'

'I'm afraid so.' Wade thumped the desk helplessly. 'This thing has been going on too long. We did not get wind of it in time. Tonight, we find slaughter right on our doorstep!'

'Do you suppose for one moment that our defence units will be asleep?' demanded the Air Ministry man. 'Do you suppose that our armies and air force will be paralysed and that this — this invader will have a walkover?'

Wade walked wearily to the window and gazed outside onto the dark bulk of the metropolis. 'I don't know,' he replied slowly. 'I have no real idea yet how far the Rutter virus has penetrated into our national system.' He looked at his watch and found that it was exactly midnight. 'We'd better — '

Suddenly the office light went out. Coupled with the blackness outside the dark was pitchy.

'What the devil!' one of the men exploded. 'What is it? Black-out regulation from the powerhouse? Or is it just a fuse gone?'

He had hardly finished speaking before a tremendous concussion, deep-seated and heavy, rolled through the night. Far away towards the harbour, flames split the ebony blackness as masonry and steel went skywards in a ragged column. A moment later there was a second explosion of equal force — and then two more. In the space of as many minutes no less than six fires were blazing in different directions, crimsoning the metropolis in lurid brilliance.

'Sabotage!' shouted the air official hoarsely, staring out. 'A signal must have been given! Explosives!'

'G-Bombs,' Turner snapped, holding his wife tightly. 'G-Bombs at a tremendous depth filled with super-powerful explosives.'

'Any way of dealing with 'em?' Wade demanded.

'Not that I know of. They're a product of atomic science and the only two men who might have controlled them — Standish, and Glebe himself — are dead.'

There was a sudden stir in the office. The officials left hurriedly for their various departments. Outside, pandemonium was rising. People were running and shouting; sirens were wailing. Out in the harbour ships hooted stridently.

'Listen!' Rita Turner exclaimed abruptly. 'Listen!'

Above the rattle and din from below, there came a dull beating, droning sound, growing increasingly louder — then in the centre of the city, right in the middle of the ring of fires, a bomb exploded with appalling violence.

'It's an air-raid!' Rita shouted. 'Bombing 'planes!'

Wade and Val Turner stared out of the window just in time to see a black fleet moving slowly against the stars. Another whine, and another tremendous explosion, and a building in the distance belched outwards and vanished in the smother.

'Why don't the defence units do something?' Rita shouted. 'Why don't they? There are no searchlights; no anti-aircraft — no defensive guided missiles! Where is everybody? Are we to stand here and be shot at?'

'Down!' Val snapped suddenly, and he pulled his wife and Wade to the floor violently. A second later a bomb exploded on the building opposite, sending a cascade of glass hurtling across the office floor. Crackling flames roared skyward and added their glare to the tumult.

The bombing 'planes were clearly visible now, deep grey in colour, with no ensign on their wings or bodies. They were circling at the moment, evidently intent on pinpointing targets, and still there was no sign of anti-aircraft fire or of interceptor 'planes or guided missiles.

'I don't understand it,' Rita whispered, shuddering. 'Why are we left helpless?'

'Pretty obvious, isn't it?' Val asked her. 'Rutter has used G-Bombs to blow up the industrial and defence points of the country, including all our missile bases. His agents must have sabotaged our nuclear submarines, too. The destruction of the powerhouses put out the lights. The air bases, the soldiers' barracks, the mobile headquarters — all the lot destroyed. Possibly he may have men of his own to take over the anti-aircraft units and they certainly won't fire on their own 'planes. The whole scheme is a masterpiece of devilish organisation.'

'But what about other countries? Our allies in NATO, for instance?' Rita demanded.

Val shrugged. 'Presumably Rutter's network of agents — all of them with access to G-Bombs — is worldwide. I don't think we can rely on help from abroad.'

'That's the way I see it, too,' Wade exclaimed. 'I knew tonight when I got that last 'phone call that we were beaten.

Those 'planes spelt the end. Maybe we deserve it.'

'A few defence units may get busy,' Val said after a moment. 'Not every defence sector and soldier in the country can be incapacitated. It just isn't feasible. And the ships around the coasts will do plenty.'

'What for instance? We don't know for certain who we're fighting, so how can we open fire on possible enemy targets?'

'I'm not referring to enemy targets. I'm referring to the time when an attempt is made to take Britain by force of arms as it will have to be finally. Terror bombing alone doesn't decide a war and when the enemy ground forces move in we may have a chance to get at 'em.'

'Which Rutter will already have thought of,' Wade sighed. 'His technique is obvious. First, terror bombing to smash morale; then his agents to hold key-centres which control light, water, electricity, tele-communications, radio, air service, food. Huh! Get rid of the idea that you have to conquer a country with land forces. You can do it by planning alone if you have a brain like Rutter's and G-Bombs to do it with.'

Wade glanced up towards the 'planes as they droned to the east of the fire-racked city.

'They've headed away for the moment,' he said. 'Now's our chance to get on the move. Safest place will be down in the Underground at the corner. Come on.'

He wrenched open the office door and Val and Rita fled after him through the deserted, smoke-filled building. In two minutes they had reached the street to find it packed with struggling shouting people, some of them with blood streaming down their faces, others searching frantically amidst fallen debris,

'Down here!' Wade snapped — and the three of them joined the mad, jostling throng crushing down the immobile escalators.

4

Aftermath

The spirit of Jonas Glebe must have viewed the results of his self-sinking bomb with bitterness. Timed to perfection and released at the vast depth specified by Rutter they performed their appalling work with crushing thoroughness. A million miles away the aliens smiled, and watched, and listened, their flawless instruments carrying to them, through complicated radio devices, the noise of a civilisation suddenly in turmoil.

In dozens of key points the industrial and defensive centres of Britain crashed inwards to become raging mines of smoke and flame. In other parts, whole army training grounds and National Militia headquarters vanished into the depths. There were also areas where spouting jets of lava belching from below had killed and maimed far more people than the actual bomb explosion.

Just as Rutter had anticipated, none of his agents was detected, and certainly none caught. Once they had started their particular lot of bombs sinking they vanished to take their place somewhere else in the relentless juggernaut of domination now fully on its way. In the main the agents scattered to anti-aircraft units to force the men in charge to hold their fire. Rutter was counting on air power and destruction of defensive weapons for his first move, and the power of the agents for the second and decisive blow. Through radio, television, and electronic communication the world heard of the sudden onslaught on Britain either in stunned amazement, or in satanic delight, depending upon who was the listener.

In the United States, girt about with rigid defence systems, there was comparative peace and quiet, but underneath it all a sense of preparedness in case the same thing happened there. Just the same, through Congress, America voiced its horror as the destruction of Britain went on unchecked, and as a gesture of sympathy a large armada of bombing 'planes and fighter aircraft was dispatched to lend assistance.

Rutter had been waiting for just such a move. Through his network the word was passed on. America had entered the fray by this move, and also depleted one of its most heavily armed centres. Now was the time for another smashing blow. The agents began to move secretly, sowing their diabolical 'eggs' as they went.

Canada, aware of Britain's desperate plight, entered the fray; pouring forth her air force across the Atlantic, trying to aid Britain to recover from the first sledge-hammer blow, but, relying on the theory that lightning attack is the key to victory, Rutter pressed on. His 'planes continued their onslaught. Destruction rained upon every city. Exploding G-Bombs took toll of all points of opposition. Canada, her attention diverted for the moment, failed to detect agents at work with further bombs within her own borders.

The British anti-aircraft guns and surviving missile bases came into action at last — but agents controlled them. Not the invading, but the Canadian and

American 'planes were shot down. Here and there a Rutter bomber was destroyed: here and there death-or-glory fliers scored a success, but futility was in the ascendant.

By day, by night, through hours which seemed hewn out of hell itself, the battle raged, Rutter directing operations by radio from his specially devised and protected underground shelter far under the now demolished Trust edifice. Little by little the remaining fighters for freedom realised that they were struggling against an enemy with an all-powerful weapon and limitless resources.

Depleted in aircraft replacements the British had not enough replacements to keep up with Rutter and his hidden factories. As fast as one of his 'planes was destroyed two more appeared to take its place.

Of the 'planes sent over the Atlantic only half survived. The rest were intercepted by the invader or by enemy warships.

Two weeks passed. The intensity of the battle began to slacken slightly. Thousands of dead and wounded lay in the smoky ruins of the British cities.

Those who were still alive crept about helplessly in blank terror of what might happen next. There seemed now to be men marching everywhere: death from the sky had apparently ceased. Just men, heavily armed, with grimly resolute faces. Many of them were Britons obeying new orders. They sent the wounded to makeshift hospitals and had the dead loaded on to trucks, but everything they did seemed to be at the point of the bayonet, and the dazed civilians obeyed because there was nothing else for it. What did seem significant was that all the men wore armlets — the armlets of European Power Cause, whatever that was supposed to mean.

★   ★   ★

Val Turner and his wife, hungry and exhausted, were wandering with the rest of the survivors through the bomb-blasted metropolis when armletted officials at last caught up with them.

What had happened to Inspector Wade was problematical. No doubt he was dead. The destruction of the Tube had sent Val and Rita pelting for safety amidst a crumbling inferno of bricks and steel and fire. Wade had been with them to begin with, but not when they had paused to look about them. They had a confused memory of living afterwards through a nightmare of explosions, of missing death by inches, until at last the onslaught had slowly abated. By the time they were captured they were too weary, physically and mentally, to even speak.

Along with hundreds of others they were thrust into a ruthlessly ransacked department store doing service as a prison. Perhaps it was days, perhaps weeks, during which they were kept alive on bread and water. Then one by one their dispirited colleagues were drafted off by the armletted men to parts unknown. So, finally, it came to their turn.

'Names?' the official asked briefly.

Val gave them indifferently and the man studied his list. Then his eyes seemed to brighten a little.

'Our Commander must see you immediately,' he said.

'Meaning Miles Rutter?' Val's smile was cynical amidst his thick blond beard.

'Naturally. Get moving!'

'And you call yourself an Englishman,' Val whispered, clenching his fists.

'A man has to live. I may as well be a guard as anything else. I've more sense than fight the inevitable. Now move!'

'Come on, Val,' Rita urged, gripping his arm. 'You can't argue with a situation like this.'

He hesitated and then shrugged his heavy shoulders. Thereafter the official piloted them through files of wearily standing men and women to a part of the ruins that had once been the City of London.

They entered by an inlet of steel and concrete a narrow passage and emerged finally in a wide underground room with its own little powerhouse for light and radio.

Miles Rutter sat at his desk. It was littered with maps and papers. At the rear stood the scrub-headed Angorstine, his lips pouting cushions. The electric clock on the wall behind him was making a satanic halo for his skull.

'The Turners,' announced the guard briefly, then with a salute he turned and went out again.

Rutter looked up with his icy grey eyes. Only his lips were smiling. 'So you didn't die after all,' he murmured. 'Well, how truly remarkable! And, in a way, most providential.'

Val waited, Rita beside him. Neither of them spoke even though they were radiating their utter contempt. Rutter still smiled.

'I gave special orders that if you were found alive you were to be brought to me. Your — er — honesty in giving your own names probably saved you from a firing squad. Nearly all the enemies of the Cause are being rounded up and shot.'

'What's so different about us?' Val asked. 'Neither of us have anything in common with a bunch of cut-throats and murderers. I speak for my wife, of course, as well as myself.'

Rita nodded her head slowly.

'Shooting,' Rutter said, 'is the quick way out. It is due to you, Turner, because you escaped prison regime by reason of the recent change in the affairs of the country. I am a just man, however, and I have decided that you shall return to prison, but certain new regulations will be enforced upon you. Your wife, because of her complicity with you in trying to expose my plans, will also go to prison. I don't want to kill you because I think it is a fitting punishment that you should both live long enough to see the changes which are going to come to Britain.'

'I was under the impression that they had already arrived,' Val remarked sourly.

'Not by any means. All over this country labour camps are being set up, and those capable of working will be drafted to them. The new Britain will be built and you two will help to build it. Every time you stumble or falter the lash will be there to remind you that there can only be one master. You will realise that you are one of the masses — you will even remember, perhaps, that you once tried to cross me!'

Again Val and Rita remained silent, both of them appalled by the vision that had risen before them, the vision of a country utterly prostrate under the heel of an invader.

'So you have nothing to say?' Rutter asked in surprise. He got to his feet and pointed to a huge world-map on the wall. 'See how we are progressing?' he asked, his eyes gleaming. 'Through war we have gained half of Europe. France and Spain are now being broken down by G-Bombs. Other bombs are at work in Southern Europe and throughout Russia and China. The far east will follow. America we have almost mastered and Canada is cracking. Once it was said that world conquest by a single power was impossible — and at that time maybe it was true. The G-Bomb changed the face of things. One scientist gave us the world — the world of power, the control of Mankind to certain tasks, which is as it should be. Free thinking is a dangerous pastime for the masses. They don't know how to use it.'

If Rutter expected a furious outburst from Val or Rita he was disappointed. Instead Val asked quietly:

'Do you honestly think that we're going to lie down under this edict? Are you idiot enough to believe that you can rule everything and meet with no opposition? Just try it, that's all. Jonas Glebe gave you the G-Bomb — but maybe that wasn't all he gave you.'

'Meaning?' Rutter snapped, a memory of Dr. Standish flashing across his brain.

Val only smiled enigmatically through his beard. Rutter glared at him for a moment and then snapped his fingers.

'Take them out,' he ordered. 'Heavy duty at Camp Four.' He watched them go, in the grip of the guards.

Angorstine said: 'You're not letting that fool Turner upset you, surely? If we have been allowed to get this far by whatever is supposed to hold the world in its fist, it is sufficient assurance that we are right. Might is right, and we've proved it. Just look here — ' With a satisfied smile he handed over a printed sheet. 'The G-Bombs are at work everywhere. Naples is undermined, and so are most parts of Canada. The capitals of the Orient, of the Far North and South. India. The Day when the Cause will rule the world is very near at hand.'

'What's this?' Rutter asked curtly. He did not seem to have heard a word of his aide's vapourings. He was looking at a totally different report.

'That?' Angorstine glanced at it. 'Oh, nothing. Just the details of a lava flow from near San Francisco. One of the G-Bomb shafts started it.'

'It did, eh?' Rutter's eyes narrowed. 'We hit a volcanic seam?'

'Possibly. One runs under America near to 'Frisco. It had a lot to do with the nineteen-hundred-and-six earth-quake, I believe, but what of it?'

'I want a geologist,' Rutter said abruptly. 'I don't care what term he is serving, who he is, but get one! There are some things I want to know about right away. Give the order to the camps, too. Find somebody with a first-class know-ledge of geology and physical sciences.'

'But I don't see — '

'Get one!' Rutter yelled, purpling.

Angorstine frowned and then went out, scratching his bullet-head. Rutter watched him go, a memory of the warning given by the murdered Standish ringing through his barbarous brain.

★　★　★

A week went by in the Labour Camp before Val and Rita fully realised what they were up against. Though separated during working hours, they found ways and means, as did the others, of getting together in the off-hours. The guards made no attempt to stop their meetings. There was no way of escape from within the railed enclosure anyway. Electrification of all barriers was possible at a moment's notice.

Day work meant ten hours of incessant hard labour in building up the ruins Rutter's air fleets had created. The former style of London buildings was, it appeared, to be excluded now in favour of long, squat edifices of a new design.

In one week Val found out plenty. Most of the camp guards were British, with a scattering of foreigners. Few of the English were brutes by nature, though they obviously had to obey orders. The laxest man of the lot was the Captain of the Guard, rather too old for his job.

Val was surprised to find that whip and gun seemed spared quite a lot, even though the ten hours labour was enforced on all males from 14 to 60. To exchange views on the regulations was to ask for trouble, but deep in Val's mind was a growing fury at the slavery, a fury fanned every time he saw his wife's drawn and weary face through the barbed wire at the quiet end of the two camps.

'Where's it all going to end, Val?' she asked him hopelessly, one night. 'The whole country, and probably the whole world before long, mowed down and sacrificed to power! It just isn't sane! It can't go on! So many against so few.'

'That isn't it,' he answered gravely. 'The few have the power, Rita, and the many have not.'

They were both mute for a moment, looking at each other in the glare of the floodlights. Around them, the everlasting propaganda from the loudspeakers shattered the air. As usual they spouted tales of conquest, some of them true, but the majority at variance with the facts Val had heard by word of mouth — little items that had escaped from the oppressed lips of suffering prisoners.

'There may be a revolt yet,' he whispered presently. 'The Captain here is pretty stupid, and there ought to be a way to get around him. There's another thing, too. You remember my telling Rutter that Glebe probably gave him something more than bombs?'

Rita nodded quickly, her eyes searching Val's face. It was grinning sardonically, as clean-shaven as his scalp now was.

'It wasn't just talk,' he breathed. 'The further Rutter and his Continental masters and agents sink the world into destruction by the indiscriminate use of G-Bombs, the nearer comes the end of the business.'

'Why? How?'

Val glanced cautiously about him and then leaned closer through the wire. 'Those bombs, as we know, have been sunk five miles down. Reports have come through from various sources that they have done more than just blast a mine in the ground. They have released volcanic forces, even in America, which is not definitely in the volcanic zone. I thought such a thing would happen because Standish mentioned it, and while I was in prison, I spent time reading geology books from the prison library. One of them said volcanic seams start at three miles down, or less. I read the books specially, as a matter of fact, thinking I might do something about it if I got out of jail. I intended, if I could, to use G-Bombs for the very purpose Rutter accidentally happened upon. Only I was going to use them to bring us victory. He's sowing world destruction — only as yet he doesn't know it.'

'But how can a few volcanic seams upset this regime?' Rita asked, puzzled.

'It's not just that: it is how long they continue which counts. Once you start to break the seals on Earth's inner forces you're letting yourself in for a whole load of trouble. Rutter has started something he can't stop — '

'Move on there!'

Rita was suddenly swung aside by a massive female guard. At the same moment Val found himself pushed away by one of her male counterparts. He wandered off, and presently found himself facing the undersized figure of Bilworthy.

Bilworthy — the little prisoner with the eyes of a rat, brightly gleaming and sinister. He gave a slow grin as he hoarded in his throat the smoke of a forbidden cigarette butt.

'Telling your wife plenty, weren't you?' he asked.

'Supposing I was?' Val eyed him bitterly. 'What the hell were you doing listening?'

'Why not? Don't we all pick up news?' Bilworthy grinned all the more and smoke escaped between his stained teeth. He shambled away rubbing his sloping, whiskery chin.

Val looked after him through slitted eyes. Three times he had encountered the slimy little prisoner poking his nose where it was not wanted. There was something about him that made Val always see red.

At last he turned away to listen to propaganda and cull from it what facts he could. Between the lines he gathered that Vesuvius was in violent eruption and hindering war activity. The bay of Naples was in the midst of the greatest lava discharge in history, and in Britain itself, an extinct volcano in the Cumberland mountains had returned to life and was belching fire and destruction for nearly fifty miles over the war-racked island. China, too, was suffering from earthquakes. In America the stubborn lava flow from the 'Frisco crater was, if anything, getting worse.

These facts were all skimmed over in the broadcast, but for Val they registered completely. He lounged over to a corner of the damp enclosure and grinned to himself. The guard who moved him on wondered vaguely what there was in Camp Four to be amused about.

Whatever plans were afoot for a revolt received an unexpected check the following morning when it was found Camp Four had a new Captain of the Guard. Val and his fellow prisoners saw the man for the first time at the line-up for building detail. Unlike his lax predecessor this individual insisted on preliminary inspection of his charges first. He walked down the line of men slowly.

He was big, possibly six-foot-three, with the shoulders and neck of a bullock. His uniform was smart and his boots polished like mirrors. His cap he wore at an angle on his shaven head. His face had square jaws and high cheekbones. His mouth slanted constantly as he talked, to reveal a line of magnificent white teeth. His eyes were blue: a cold, hard blue.

'From what I hear there has been too much sentiment around here,' he shouted, walking along deliberately. 'Too much!' He looked at the dull faces, and his short whip swung at his hip. 'I'm going to change all that from now on. I've been a soldier all my life, see? I know what men need to make 'em work, and that's discipline! Discipline! From me you'll get it as never before. We're building an Empire here for the Cause, and you dogs will work ten hours a day to the full whilst I'm in charge. Ten hours

— no more, no less. I know my duty, and I perform it. My name is Abel Granvort, your new Captain of the Guard, better known as 'Ox'. Later on you'll find out why! All right, Sergeant Mead, take over.'

The file, with the guards around them, shambled off, but as Val marched, the Ox shot out his hand and took him to one side.

'Not you,' he said briefly. 'I want a word with you, Turner.'

Val waited, eyeing the man steadily.

'So you think Leader Rutter is digging his own grave do you?'

Val's eyes travelled to the undersized back of Bilworthy as he tramped away with the others.

'I spoke!' Ox bellowed.

'Yes, I heard you,' Val said calmly, turning back to him. 'I suppose Bilworthy's been opening his mouth wide again, eh? Amazing what some people will do. To answer your question, though; yes, I do think that Rutter and his bunch of murderers are heading for disaster. Do you feel like making something of it?'

'Come with me, Turner! March!' Ox's

shiny boots set the pace through the dust.

Val found himself taken to camp headquarters. Ox left him and stood aside at poker-like attention. Rutter was present with the inevitable thick-lipped Angorstine

Rutter came straight to the point: 'Last night, Turner, I understand that you had a conversation with your wife amounting pretty close to treason. That was why I had the guard tightened up, and put Captain Granvort in charge! You had the impudence to tell your wife that we are destroying our regime by our own hand. What have you to say?'

'Nothing,' Val answered coldly.

'You realise I can have you flogged and then shot? Your wife too?'

At that Ox stepped forward. 'I submit, sir that the woman had nothing to do with it. She was the recipient of the information, involuntarily — not the giver. Therefore according to military regulations she — '

'Shut up!' Rutter roared in fury. 'Get back to your place and don't speak until you're spoken to — Now you!' He swung back to Val. 'I could kill both you and your wife, but if you will give me some information I will spare you both, and see that you have lighter duties.'

'We don't want favours,' Val retorted; then he reflected for a moment. 'At least, I don't; but I have my wife to consider. What do you want to know?'

'I believe you know something of geology?'

'Average. I certainly haven't the knowledge of the late Doctor Standish.'

'At least you have more than I, and I am prepared to admit it. When you were my secretary, you gave many revelations of your intellect. At the moment geologists and scientists are hard to find; so many of them have been disposed of. You seem to know something judging from what you had to say to your wife. It is common knowledge now that severe volcanic eruptions are taking place everywhere, and many of my friends in Europe — some of them my superiors — have demanded to know how these troubles can be stopped.'

'They blame me because I instituted the G-Bomb. Earthquakes and landslides are seriously impeding Army operations. Heavy fogs are beginning to cover the seas from the intense heat at the ocean floor. That hinders air work. Rivers, filled with flowing lava, are drying up. You told your wife you read of the possibility of all this happening whilst you were in prison. In that case you may know how to stop it?'

'In other words, you're getting frightened?'

'Answer my question!'

'All right. There is no way to stop it. If there were I'd tell you — not because I have any regard for you, but in the interests of human beings generally. You sank your G-Bombs too deep, that's all. Later on, seams will open in the ocean beds and the fun will begin in real earnest. The water will pour into the gaps. Immense steam pressure will gather underground and blow chasms in the earth.' Val paused and smiled bitterly. 'What you and your butchers actually started was the end of the world! You're getting the world, sure — just as you wanted — but you'll perish with it like the rest of us, for us it doesn't matter much because death is preferable to being ruled by you and yours.'

If Rutter was disturbed he did not show it. His voice was as hard as steel when he spoke again: 'You mean you won't help us?'

'I've told you the truth. Take it or leave it.'

'I don't believe you,' Rutter said flatly, and turned to look at Ox. 'Return him to the Camp, Captain, and deliver twenty-five lashes each day for a week. At the end of that time he may choose to speak more freely. For the moment his wife will escape the lash: later I may not be so lenient. It is up to you now, Turner.'

'You infernal — ' Val started to shout, then Ox whirled him outside.

'Wait a minute!' Val cried, tearing himself free. 'I've got plenty more to tell that hyena! I — '

'Move!' Ox commanded inexorably, whipping out his gun. 'Quick march!'

Helplessly Val turned and marched back to the workers on the building job. Once there he waited for the shirt to be ripped from his back and the flogging to commence.

'Well, what in blazes are you standing there for?' Ox demanded, and Val turned in surprise.

'Rutter said — '

'To work!' Ox commanded, pointing with his gun. 'Rutter ordered me to flog you. Regulation nineteen of a soldier's duty says a Captain can give orders but shall not execute them personally. That is for lesser ratings to do. Leader Rutter gave me an order I could not carry out. I know my duty and I do it, but that won't save you doing your ten hours,' he finished with a sneer. 'Ten hours! No more — no less. Now get busy!'

Val turned, astounded at the rigid adherence of the man to rules and regulations. He seemed to be a brute by nature with Clauses A to Z branded on his brain, yet somehow he made Val smile. As he worked he studied him, standing motionless, with feet apart and hands on hips, a twisted grin on his square face.

Then Val looked at somebody else. Bilworthy.

5

The Ark

Not even the stranglehold of censorship could entirely disguise the news leaking in during the ensuing days. A foggy steam settled over Britain and palled the Labour Camps completely. The guard was doubled and the fence electrified to make escape impossible. Heat, too, smote the country like a white-hot bar. Reports came in of Etna, Vesuvius, Stromboli, Fujiyama, and other famous volcanoes going full blast. Smoke and scorching dust from their vigorous craters was penetrating into the atmosphere and producing the most extraordinary sunlight whenever it was glimpsed. The sky seemed to be mixed with blue and magenta colourings through high dust film.

From Italy came the report of the total destruction of Sardinia and Corsica through volcanic eruption. Molten lava pouring into the sea had turned the Bay of Naples into a death cauldron, paralysing shipping, giving up dead and bloated fish and driving poisonous fumes across the Italian and south European lands. The whole southern end of the Italian peninsula indeed seemed to be sinking under the scalding sea.

In two places in the Atlantic fissures had occurred across the ocean floor creating incredible havoc. Swollen with steam pressure, whole masses of ocean bed had blown up and driven a wilderness of raging steam and water before them. Earthquakes in mid-Europe and Asia, lava floods in parts of the Himalayas that menaced India and vast parts of Mongolia, had started an exodus of refugees greater than was produced by the war itself.

The already filled Labour Camps in the conquered countries began to swell to overflowing with unending streams of survivors from all manner of climes. In Camp Four alone the course of one day saw the addition of a thousand prisoners, some of them dark-skinned men and women of the East who had caught the last surviving boats from their doomed lands and sought the apparent safety of Britain, only to drop into the hands of human foes instead.

All the time the aliens surveyed the scene and congratulated themselves. Constantly, night and day, the master-telescope was kept trained upon the Earth, and when the aliens were not present — due to the need of rest or nourishment — automatic sound-cameras recorded everything which the screen had to show. The vision of chaos was something that made even the unemotional Leader of aliens smile in satisfaction.

'I think my friends, there is little doubt that we shall achieve our object,' he commented. 'The man Glebe reacted just as we hoped he would, and Miles Rutter is carrying his ambition beyond the bounds of prudence, as we believed he would. Yes, in but a little while we shall have that Earth exactly as we want it, a world in ruin with a few straggling survivors who will be unable to face the brief but decisive onslaught we shall launch. To conquer a world before you even set foot on it is scientific planning indeed.'

'I wish,' one of the expedition remarked, 'I could feel as confident as you, sire. I still have the feeling — as at first — that sooner or later some Earthling with more intellect than the others will arise and handle this desperate situation, and so bring about the defeat of our plan.'

The Leader frowned. 'I deplore your pessimism, my friend, and always have done. Throughout your scientific career you have been one to search for the unknown factor, the one to spread gloom in the midst of joyous achievement. Laudable in its place, but not to be overdone.'

'My humble apologies,' the other murmured. 'I only speak as I feel, and logic will not permit me to accept the idea that every Earthling is so witless as to be unable to destroy, or at least neutralise, the elemental upheaval with which he is now faced. With all deference, sire, I would suggest a further reading of surviving Earthlings, now their numbers are so very much thinned, to discover if there are any with sufficient brain-power to prove a menace.'

'And if we did find such a person, or persons?' the Leader asked irritably. 'What then?'

'Something might be arranged for that person to be removed. We cannot afford to take chances at this stage in our plans.'

The Leader hesitated, then turned to the huge panel of instruments, the attentive crew gathered around him.

He half reached out a tentaculate hand towards the instrument for determining Earthly mental rating, and then he paused.

'No!' he snapped. 'No, I won't waste time on such a useless cause, my friends. We have much to do planning our journey to Earth when the final catastrophe assails them: I do not propose to waste valuable weeks searching for a brilliant mind which I am convinced does not exist there.'

The dignitaries glanced at one another, but there was nothing they could do because the decision of the Leader was absolute; so they watched the screen instead and considered in complacent silence the death-throes of a planet. The view was a fairly distant one, encompassing most of Earth turned at that period towards them: certainly it was not pin-pointed particularly on Camp Four in Britain, otherwise the aliens would have been interested in Val Turner, in the midst of trying to pacify the more unruly spirits about him.

'We have got to revolt!' one of the men shouted, standing on an upturned box in the midst of the tin-roofed dormitory where the men were gathered for the night preparatory to 'lights out'.

'Right! There's no other way.'

'You told us the G-Bombs caused all this, Val. The whole world is cracking up — rivers and seas evaporating — and we sit here and take it! If we're to save our lives, we've got to smash this regime once and for all!'

Val looked up thoughtfully and then said: 'To revolt, Hoyle, is the surest way to lose our lives, not save them.'

'Then what do we do?' Hoyle spat. 'Sit here until we fry or something? The heat gets worse every day. We sweat, and build, and sweat some more, and that grinning swine Ox looks on and revels in every minute of it. It can't go on! What's more it isn't going to — '

'Now listen to me, boys.' Val got to his feet from sitting on his bunk and faced the grim-faced crowd. 'Listen to me for a moment. I've told you the truth every time so far, haven't I? I predicted this would happen even though you rather doubted it at the time, eh?'

'Yes, that's right,' one of the men admitted. 'All the same, I agree with Hoyle that it's time we got some kind of action against Rutter. The war is finished now by this upheaval of Nature, and Rutter and his gang are left masters of the world quicker than they expected. Are we going to sit down to that?'

'For the time being, yes,' Val replied flatly.

'But why?' Hoyle pleaded. 'Where's the sense of it?'

'I'll tell you why. Believe me, in a while these vast volcanic upheavals will cease — they are bound to find a new level. In that time something will happen. Seas and rivers are evaporating at top speed — but did any of you stop to think where all the steam is going? Not all of it is included in this world-mist by any means.'

'What's that got to do with our revolt?' Hoyle shouted.

'Just this: The conditions which existed at the beginning of the world are being repeated through a blunder of Rutter's own making! In the early days of Earth vast heat drove colossal clouds of steam and vapour way out beyond the atmospheric limits. It formed into a ring around the Earth drawn into that position by centrifugal force. A titanic vapour girdle wrapping the Earth about as, today, the rings of Saturn girdle that giant planet. Today, the driven steam from rivers and seas and lakes will do the same thing. The outer part of the ring will be frozen by space; the inner part will still be vapour by reason of the Earth's heat, after a while the girdle will be drawn back to Earth.'

'Then what?' Hoyle asked, in a quieter voice.

'Then — the Deluge!' Val answered gravely. 'A world swept clean with only a scattering of survivors. That is where this insane drive for domination is going to end. Maybe a few who are left will be able to build on better lines.'

The assembled men looked at one another rather blankly; then they all started talking at once. They quieted again at the voice of a little, leathery-faced Mongolian who had been sitting passively listening. Now he spoke, in perfect English.

'You are quite right, my young friend, but you put it badly,' he commented. 'My name, incidentally, is Kang. I was driven here from Mongolia by disasters beyond the memory of man being again repeated. I foresaw, long ago, that the present happenings would repeat themselves in a Deluge.'

He looked around at his listeners — a wizened creature with a face like ancient parchment. In his oblique eyes there was a depth of wisdom seen in very few men.

'It is,' he continued, 'a matter of geological history that the vapours ascended while the Earth was hot, and cooled into the Deluge as Earth cooled — just as they will do on this occasion. In Jupiter we behold today vast canopies around that planet in the form of cloud belts. So must Earth have looked once. Proof of the original Deluge is imprinted forever in the legends and histories of nations.'

'For instance?' Hoyle asked, rather dryly.

The Mongolian shrugged. 'Consider the Japanese Bible — the *Kojiki*, which refers to a 'floating bridge in Heaven where live the Gods'. On the other hand, Veruna — which as all Sanskrit scholars know was the primitive Indian Heaven of the Vedas — means, when translated, 'Watery Heaven'. Again, Scandinavian history refers to a 'Bridge of Heaven which broke through', and does not your own Bible refer frequently to 'the waters above and the waters below'? Yes, my friends, there was a Deluge.'

'Yes,' Hoyle admitted, startled by his fellow-worker's scholarly knowledge. 'Yes, I think you may be right, Kang.'

'I am right, otherwise I would not have spoken.'

There was silence for a while. The statements of the gnome-like intellectual had proved rather overpowering. Val was the first to recover.

'From the rate at which evaporation has gone on,' he continued, 'it is possible that the return of the waters to Earth when the cooling-off begins may produce a flood which will cover the world! Even a rainfall of fifteen feet in the space of forty days and forty nights — like the early Deluge — would produce a flood transcending our imagination, and this one threatens to be even worse.'

''I do bring a Flood of waters on the Earth', Genesis, sixth chapter, seventeenth verse,' Kang murmured, closing his eyes in meditation.

'Yes, and what do we do?' Hoyle shouted.

'That's easy,' growled a worker at the back. 'We sit in this camp and get drowned.'

'No we don't,' Val said slowly. 'We do the same thing as Noah did — build an Ark!'

He was conscious of a passing surprise

at his own statement. He had not even thought of the notion a moment before. Yet now it seemed logical and obvious.

'This ain't the time to get funny!' Hoyle snapped.

'I mean it!' Val insisted. 'We're building edifices, aren't we? What's to prevent us building an edifice as an Ark instead of a building? That's it!' he went on, snapping his fingers. 'The buildings are all long, beetling ones, able to hold about five-hundred people when empty. We'll go on building just as we have been doing — but we'll make the edifice moveable and able to float when the waters come. Nobody — not even Ox — will notice the difference. In fact outwardly there won't be a difference.'

Voices buzzed. 'Maybe he's got something?'

'It can't miss.'

'You have a wise friend and leader amongst you,' Kang observed, opening his eyes again. 'Heed him. He has the spirit and energy of a deliverer.'

The men nodded resolutely. Val looked at them earnestly in turn, reading loyalty to him — until he came to the face of Bilworthy. As Val's keen gaze fell upon him Bilworthy shambled off towards his crude bunk.

Val's hand dropped on his shoulder. 'Just a moment, Bilworthy!' Val swung him round. 'You squealed on me last time to Ox. I let it pass on that occasion because it didn't do me much actual harm. If you repeat one word of what has been said here tonight I'll get you. Or one of us will. Understand?'

'Now — now why should I — '

'Understand?' Val demanded ominously.

'Yes. Yes, I under — understand.' Bilworthy turned away scowling. Then the door opened and the guard came in vigorously.

'Lights out; you scum! Hurry it up there!'

★　★　★

When, some weeks later, the world-wrapping mists began to rise and there came reports of abating volcanic eruptions, Rutter began to breathe a little more freely, but not for long. With Angorstine he decided to investigate for himself the lack of fresh orders from Continental headquarters, and it was the aeroplane trip that rammed home the appalling truth to his brain.

The Atlantic Ocean had dropped tremendously in its level. Here and there ships were nosing through channels foreign to maritime knowledge. In other places vessels had broken their backs or lay bleached and forlorn with their sides rusting. The British Isles, still filled with hurrying, desperate people in the war-cracked cities, were perched up like mountain tops a thousand feet or so above sea level. Cliffs never seen before had come to light.

Europe provided its own explanation for lack of orders from G.H.Q. of the Cause. One half of the great European plain from mid-Russia to mid-Germany was nothing but a lava-field, hardened now, from which poked the shattered remnants of buildings. People, in little bunches, were gathered around crude camps before smoky fires. It was a glimpse of the troglodyte age. Civilisation in Europe was ended.

Dazed, too stunned to understand the portent of it all, Rutter had the 'plane pilot continue the trip. By degrees the whole globe was circumnavigated and the tale of tragedy unreeled. Everywhere there seemed to be either lava-fields, dried-up rivers, or depleted oceans. Shipping was obviously doomed. Parts of the air were thick with either battering tempests or poisonous volcanic fumes. Occasionally through the driving reek there was a vision of a grey belt girdling the heavens. Very much sobered, Rutter returned to his London headquarters.

'Angorstine,' he said slowly, 'there is only one governing mind left in the Cause, and that is mine! The others are all dead. Obviously it becomes necessary to plan the world afresh with you and I at the head of it.'

'I'm always at your side, sir,' Angorstine answered promptly.

'Purely for what you can get out of it, my friend, and I am not deluded into thinking otherwise. However, it's clear that we can overcome the few survivors with ease. We can make the workers in these Labour Camps build as they have never built before. That is what we will do! Chance has destroyed all those with whom I worked, and it has made me alone master of the world.'

This time Angorstine did not comment. He was looking out of the window onto the grey band across the sky. 'I wonder what that is?' he asked musingly.

Rutter gave an impatient movement. 'Stop wasting time on trifles and summon the guard. I have new regulations to put into force. Buildings must be hurried to completion. Several batches of workers must be drafted overseas to commence work there, and we must also make arrangements to conserve water. It is becoming a problem.'

'Maybe Turner could explain that grey band?' Angorstine suggested, turning.

'What the devil do you keep worrying about that for?' Rutter demanded. 'Didn't you hear what I said?'

'Yes, sir, I did — but I'd still like that phenomenon in the sky explained. It isn't natural, and things that aren't natural always worry me.'

'Then stop worrying and give your mind to your job. As for Turner, forget him.'

'Why, sir? You said yourself he's a fairly good man when it comes to intellect, yet you never summoned him to you again after giving that order to have him flogged.'

'No use sending for him: he's too stubborn. Besides there are more important matters. Get a move on, man!'

Angorstine saluted, and went, and it was mainly through him that the news got around that Rutter had become undisputed master of the world. Not that this made any impression on the prisoners in the camps. Things could not get much worse for them in any case. Water was rationed, and precious little there was of it. Food was usually dry bread interspersed with vegetable concoctions from the fast dying fields. Whatever worthwhile there was left in the eating line found its way to Rutter, Angorstine and a few others in charge.

Despite the privations, Val and his colleagues worked on steadily, keeping their eyes upon that grey band that daily became larger in the sky. Otherwise the sky was rainless, blue, and sunny. Only that grey arc of slowly returning vapour revealed what was coming. Val wondered if Rita was watching it too. Communication with her was difficult these days; At least she was still alive; Val knew that much, and she knew too that an Ark was intended.

Carrying out the plan they had arranged, Val and his co-workers constructed one of the new buildings to their own design, providing it with a keel, and watertight floor, and apparently nobody was any the wiser. The guards had certainly no reason to suspect any trickery. Yes, everything seemed to be working out very nicely, except, for the lack of water.

Working ten hours a day in blazing sunshine and dust with lips cracked and muscles aching told upon the strongest constitution, but Ox allowed no let up. He had permitted himself only the same ration as the prisoners, apparently regarding the camp as a beleagured fortress. He was always at his post, intent on every aspect of his duty.

A grinding, merciless month slipped by. In that time the grey band in the sky had crept nearer and nearer, drawn by the cooling Earth. Landscapes, lava-caked and hard now, were wilted with sunshine. Underneath them lay the buried fields and pastureland, gone probably for ever. Even Miles Rutter was wondering if he could ever establish a new empire out of this cracked, battered wilderness of his own making, from which rain seemed to have eternally departed.

The detachments of prisoners he had sent overseas were dying, said reports — dying of thirst or else starvation. Others were being preyed upon by the cannabalistic survivors of the eruptions in mid-Europe.

Only those in Camp Four knew what was really coming, and it gave them cause enough to smile through their flaked lips. Water! There would be more than enough before long! Water without ceasing, and Building Number Seven all ready to float. All it needed now was a thorough examination, in order to check its watertight qualities, and then provisioning. These two were big problems.

At intervals, when opportunity seemed favourable, Val slipped out to pass news to his wife. On one of the nights he was followed by the shadowy figure of Bilworthy, but Bilworthy went in the opposite direction, licking his parched lips as he went. At length he reached the door of Ox's guardroom and knocked softly. After a moment the door swung open.

'Well, what do you want?' Ox stood glaring down, his great figure silhouetted by the oil light behind him. Power, relying on water for its generation, had ceased long since.

'I — I've something more to tell you, sir. It's worth a can of water. That's all I ask.' Bilworthy stood sliding his palms down his overalls.

'You get your ration,' Ox retorted. 'We all get half a pint a day — no more, no less.' He seemed to ponder, then suddenly shooting out his arm he pulled the scrawny little prisoner to him, up the steps, and into the guard-room. Here a final twist flung Bilworthy across the floor. He crouched, half afraid.

'I hate the sight of you but I may as well listen,' Ox said, perching himself on the edge of the rough table. 'What have you got to say this time?'

'It's — it's about that prisoner Turner,' Bilworthy panted, fingering his lips nervously as he regained his feet. 'He's plotting treason again.'

'Oh, he is?' Ox's eyes slitted. 'How?'

'He's building an Ark.'

'He's building a what?'

'An Ark. Like the one Noah did — He says there's a Deluge coming! That grey band in the sky is water and it's going to come back to Earth.'

'Oh, so that's what that grey band is? Well — go on, and don't miss anything or I'll kick your face in.'

By degrees, his voice hoarse with both drought and excitement, Bilworthy got out every part of the story. At the end of the narrative Ox stood up, calmly drew on his shiny boots, donned his coat, and then pointed to the door.

'Outside, you rat. Show me this Ark

— and you'd better be right!'

Bilworthy looked longingly at the water tank. 'A — about some water, Captain — I — I can hardly speak.'

'You don't need to after all you've had to say. You'll get your water later. I mean to be sure first. Come on.'

Ox bundled the hapless Bilworthy down the steps, and he kept a grip on his collar as he marched him across the camp grounds and out to the building site. When they came to Building Number Seven Ox marched inside and flashed on his torch. Ten minutes of minute examination convinced him. He emerged into the open again and stood speculating.

'I — I was right, wasn't I?' Bilworthy urged, clutching at him. 'Room enough in here for nearly five-hundred people. It will float too — '

'I've got eyes of my own,' Ox broke in, 'and get your filthy hands off me! I'm particular.'

With a twitch of his powerful arm he sent Bilworthy spinning backwards; then he took his whistle from his pocket and blew it stridently. After a while hastily-dressed guards came running up in the starlight.

'Summon every prisoner in the camp out here,' Ox commanded. 'At the double!'

There was an immediate scurrying and blowing of more whistles. Ox stood waiting, his feet apart and hands on hips, as the men in their coarse nightshirts came stumbling along in their bare feet, finally forming into a rough column. Val, his lips set in a taut line, stood gazing at Bilworthy's cringing form immediately behind Ox.

'Men,' Ox said deliberately, unfastening his whip from his belt and flexing it in his powerful hands, 'I pride myself that I have treated you with the justice of a soldier whilst I have been here. Right?'

Heads nodded slowly.

'I'm a hard man — ' Ox descended the steps of Building Number Seven and began to walk along the line of men.

'I'm a hard man, I say, but that is because I obey orders to the letter. There is a code of honour amongst true soldiers, even as there is amongst prisoners and workers. Right here is a man who tries to sell the lot of you for an extra can of water!'

Ox swung and spat in the dust straight

at Bilworthy's feet. Bilworthy had been creeping along in the rear of Ox's great form, more for protection than anything else.

Now he stood staring, taken aback by Ox's about-face.

'But — but, Captain, you promised me — '

'Yes, I promised you water,' Ox assented. 'You'll get it, but it won't do you any good. You're a skunk, Bilworthy. You squealed once, and now you've squealed again just to try and get more than your share! To try and get more than the prisoners, and more than the guards!'

'So he told you about the Ark?' Val asked grimly.

'About the Ark and about the Deluge. I'll deal with that later. As for you, Bilworthy, I've only one punishment for a prisoner who sells his comrades, and tries to get more than he's entitled to.' Ox stopped playing with his whip abruptly and whirled it round. The biting thongs flayed the torn shirt from Bilworthy's back. He fell in the dust, howling.

'Water!' he screeched. 'That's all I wanted! Just a drop of water!'

'A can full,' Ox agreed, and his whip split the silence again. 'Salty, stinking water — the sweat of your own filthy hide as you crawl from this lash. Go on — crawl! Crawl!'

Time and again the lash came round with pistol-shot force. The prisoners stood motionless, themselves sweating, wincing at every swing of that mighty arm. Groaning, dragging himself in the dust, Bilworthy crawled into a corner by the Ark building. Ox stopped then and ground the moistured drops from Bilworthy under the heel of his shiny boot.

'I'm not reporting this because it is the only thing you could think up to save us from the coming Deluge,' Ox announced curtly. 'I am not reporting it — yet. You're going to finish it properly first, make a thorough job of it. You are going to fit steering-gear, provision it, give it paddle-power — which you can all provide by physical labour. Like they did on the old slave-ships, remember? Because you decided to build it, you'll be allowed to travel in it — at a price — and it's to your credit that you'll save the Leader of us all when the Flood comes.'

'You mean Rutter comes into the Ark too?' Val shouted,

'He's the Leader, and he comes — with Angorstine,' Ox snapped. 'You found the way out, and we'll sail under Rutter when the skies open. You'll finish this Ark under my orders. Ten hours a day — no more, no less. Now, dismiss!'

Val hesitated, his fists clenched; then the small brown hand of Kang clutched at his arm.

'Do as he says, my friend,' he whispered. 'He is only obeying his highest sense of duty. No man, whatever his beliefs, can do more.'

'*But Rutter* — !' Val was aghast.

'Move!' Ox bellowed. 'You too!' He caught up the cringing, nearly naked figure of Bilworthy and hurled him into the line. 'Quick march! Never mind the stones. Think yourselves lucky you've got feet at all!' His polished boots flashed as he set the pace.

6

Deluge

The next day the sun was obscured for the first time in many weeks and the whole of the sky looked like a great inverted bowl of grey lowering down to Earth.

Eased a little by the absence of sunshine, but still physically weary to the breaking point, Val and the others went to work exclusively on the Ark. Most of the men were bitter, rebellious at having to accept the idea of Rutter joining them. Neither did they listen with good grace to the counsel of the little Mongolian who seemed to see some sort of virtue in the straddle-legged giant in the shiny boots who tirelessly watched over them.

Obeying his orders, a system of paddles was devised and seats were fixed inside the Ark building for the hapless ones who would have to wield the oars. Rough beds were made too, and chairs and tables.

There were movable stands for oil lamps so they'd stand upright under all circumstances. Floodlights, to act as searchlights, operating from batteries, were installed. Amongst a multitude of other things the interior of the Ark was partitioned. It was evident that Ox had possible women survivors in mind and meant to keep things in order.

★   ★   ★

Four days passed, in which Miles Rutter tried to work out ways and means of saving his crumbling empire. Unofficial reports had reached him from long-distance fliers that Europe was experiencing rain. It made him smile and feel more comfortable. Once the problem of water was solved, he would soon tighten his grip again.

Over Britain, drifting from Europe, the clouds lowered all through the intervening days and nights and in every camp the prisoners were working in twilight gloom. Then as they finished work on the evening of the fourth day little spots of moisture started dropping on their barely covered backs and spattered in the dust.

'Rain!' one of the men shrieked. 'Rain!'

He stood with his face upturned to the black sky, mouth open to catch the drops. Then Ox's mighty fist hurled him into the line of men. 'Keep marching, you! You'll get your bellyful later! Now march!'

Spots of wet and splashes of mud marred Ox's immaculate boots as he herded the line back to camp. Once there he stood with arms akimbo appraising the blackness overhead. Turning presently he saw Val staring upwards too.

'Looks like you were right, Turner,' he said briefly. 'Get inside.'

Within the long building Val was immediately met with a barrage of questions. The presence of the guards was ignored. For that matter they were as interested as the prisoners in impending events.

'Is it coming, Val?' Hoyle demanded. 'Is it the Deluge beginning?'

'Yes, my friends, the Deluge,' answered Kang, from his corner, 'the last hours of a phase of brutal power domination are here. Be assured that we shall find safety in the end.'

'I wish I could be assured,' Val said anxiously, as the pattering rain increased to a sudden fierce drumming on the roof. 'This has been gathering for weeks — seas and rivers returning — '

'Hey, you men!' Ox stood in the doorway again with water trickling down his chin. 'Outside and drink your fill, the whole perishing lot of you! Some of the holes have filled up with water. Hurry it up!'

He cracked his whip to accelerate the scramble outside. As Bilworthy came scurrying past Ox delivered a terrific kick that sent the little man crashing on his face in the mud outside. He got up again, elbowed an elderly prisoner out of the way from the nearest hole, and drove his face into the pool.

Something blazed through the dark — the explosion of Ox's gun. Bilworthy relaxed, his head sunk under the water. For a moment there was silence. Then Ox came slowly down the dripping steps, lifted Bilworthy's corpse out of the mud and threw it to one side as though it were a wet sack. He motioned to the trembling old man.

'Go on, granddad, drink,' he ordered; then looking at the rest of the men he bawled, 'I'll have every man here drink his fill — no more, no less, and I'll shoot any man who tries to get more than his share! Now hurry it up,' he added urgently as the rain increased in force.

At last the men were satisfied, and came stumbling through the blinding torrent back to the camp. Ox followed them, surveying their dripping forms for a moment, and then said curtly: 'No man moves out of here to that Ark until I give the order. Understood?' He went out and slammed the door.

★   ★   ★

On the alien spaceship the Leader was troubled, so much so he had paused in the midst of making preparations for the journey to Earth, to study his apparatus. As usual his fellows were around him, not in the least understanding the problem that was evidently preoccupying the mastermind of the race,

'I don't understand it,' the Leader

declared at last, his brows knitted. 'It isn't as though the instrument is out of order for it registers all other people on Earth except that one.'

'To whom are you referring, Master?' one of the aliens asked.

'Haven't I told you?' The Leader looked surprised for a moment and then shook his head. 'Why no, of course not. I had forgotten. Let me show you.'

He adjusted the telescopic apparatus, and after a while there appeared on the screen a somewhat dimly lighted image of a small, brown-faced man with oblique eyes. He was squatting on his haunches, apparently meditating.

'That is the being I cannot fathom,' the Leader muttered. 'He has, as you know, made many statements recently to the fools gathered around him, and he is obviously a creature of no mean intelligence. In fact he is far more intelligent than the majority of Earthlings. Yet he does not register a mental quotient! All my efforts to get his mental status point to zero. See for yourselves.'

The Leader switched on the sensitive

mechanism, but the needle remained completely unresponsive — yet when trained on any of the other men around the main subject it reacted normally.

'Strange,' the Leader mused. 'Extremely strange!'

'I would consider it more than just strange, sire,' commented the alien who had been accused of being pessimistic. 'I would be more inclined to consider it a portent.'

'A portent? Of what?'

'Catastrophe, as far as we are concerned. There is an Earthling there clever enough to offset us when we try to read his mental energy. That seems to suggest he knows of us, and maybe of our plans.'

'Absurd! He could not.'

The alien was silent, his eyes on the screen. Around him his colleagues looked at each other. Then one of them said:

'May we have again a recording of what he has said in the past, sire? Perhaps something may be gleaned from it.'

'If you wish,' the Leader responded, turning to the sound apparatus. 'Though I don't think we will learn much. That particular Earthling is utterly inscrutable.

He calls himself Kang of Mongolia and for some reason seems able to anticipate exactly what is going to happen on Earth. I am not at all cheered by the fact that he has not foreseen our advent on Earth.'

'Possibly,' said the pessimist, 'because there will be no advent. We cannot afford to tackle the unknown factor in a project as important as ours, sire.'

The Leader fixed the recording apparatus to his liking and then turned, his eyes sharp.

'I have warned you on previous occasions, my friend, about your pessimism concerning an unknown factor! Let there be no more of it. Even if there is an unknown factor we shall have to face it because migration to Earth is our only chance of survival — Ah, now let us hear what this individual Kang said.'

The others became silent, listening over again to the observations of the Mongolian. The recording was mainly concerned with his statements upon the Deluge and his various historical proofs of the cataclysm having happened once before in the dawn of Earth's life. When the recording was finished the aliens looked at one another questioningly.

'There is nothing to be gained from that,' one of them said decisively. 'The creature is simply one of the millions teeming on Earth and conveys the impression of great intelligence — even prescience — because he is well read. Certainly I do not see any reason to be disturbed, sire.'

'Then can you explain why we cannot get his mental energy quotient?' the Leader demanded.

'I can think of one possible reason,' another said. 'If at some time he has had a head operation — surgical treatment of some kind, maybe — it is possible that a plate of metal may be in his skull over the brain. That would prevent his thought emanations being given off with enough power for our detectors to receive them.'

The Leader reflected, looking surprised, then he nodded slowly. 'Yes, that is one possibility. The other one I have already mentioned — that he knows what we are trying to do.'

'Most unlikely, sire. The presence of our vessel can hardly be suspected, so far away are we. I am perfectly sure no Earthling has instruments powerful enough to detect us.'

'Yes — as far as Earthlings are concerned,' the Leader admitted. 'But I wonder if — other worlds — ?'

The others started slightly. It was a fact that, so concentrated were they upon the destruction of Earth's peoples, to enable them to assume easy control of the planet, that they had never given a thought to the other worlds in the Earth's solar system. The earlier probe had, of course, studied every one of them upon first entering the system, and recorded all that was discovered about them, before settling into an orbit around the Earth.

He operated a keyboard, and within a short time, the central computer displayed the relevant data upon a large screen.

'There is no life on any of the other worlds,' remarked the pessimist, after studying the screen display. 'Not that the probe could detect, anyway. The nearest to the sun is a blistered and frozen sepulchre; the next nearest is empty — a hothouse desert of a world, with dense poisonous clouds, through which, fortunately, our apparatus can penetrate. Then comes Earth and afterwards another dead planet of cratered deserts and attenuated atmosphere. As for the outer worlds — '

'Yes, the outer worlds,' the Leader broke in, thinking. 'The temptation is to dismiss those distant rolling worlds, believing them so frigid and poisonous to be hardly worth profound study. Yet perhaps we have been foolish, for if you consider it, we see in each of those outer worlds conditions very similar to those now existent on Earth Dense cloud banks, banded layers of vapour.' He stopped, lost in thought.

'I fail to see the connection, sire,' one of the aliens remarked finally, and at that the Ruler looked up sharply.

'The connection is this: On the distant planets a Deluge is a common thing. It is all part and parcel of those planets' particular state of development, which means that any inhabitants of those planets will be accustomed to Deluge conditions and know how to handle them. Well then, let us assume that one of those denizens has taken it into his head to help the people of Earth in their plight. That would mean a being who does not register on our instruments — mentally at least — because the instruments are set for Earth beings only.'

'An interesting theory, sire, but I cannot conceive of the inhabitant of another planet being so anxious to help Earth people in their present dilemma. Why should he?'

'Sentiment — pure and simple. We of this world have long since outgrown all emotions, sentiment amongst them, but I am quite sure some such emotionally-directed being might attempt to help Earthlings to survive.'

'And destroy our hopes.'

'Delay them certainly. I shall only regard our hopes destroyed if the survivors are numerous, and capable of rebuilding their civilisation. What we require are only a few thousand left — none at all if possible — and reduce those few to the status of workers so they will obey the commands we give them. Then it will be simple,'

'So,' the pessimistic alien said, 'we either

face a being of another planet — who must have a high intelligence in order to have crossed space — or else somebody who is an Earthling but unexpectedly intellectual and able to stop us reading his mental quotient, either by accident or design. What is the answer, sire?'

'Destroy him,' another alien said promptly, and earned a bitter look from the Leader.

'Destroy him? How? How, when his mind is a solid wall which we cannot break down? We cannot give him mental orders and at this distance we cannot produce physical effects that might encompass his destruction. He is safe from us. We have two alternatives, either to leave for Earth immediately and, in the midst of the confusion of this coming Deluge, find the Ark and annihilate it; or examine the first of the outer planets, the biggest one of all, carefully and see if any beings resembling this Kang do exist upon it. If so we can tap their mental radiations and determine the correct wavelength for affecting their type of brain. Plainly, a study of the giant world is the easiest first course.'

'I don't agree,' another said. 'It would

be simpler to travel to Earth and locate this Ark. From what we have heard it is the only one of its kind, and contains the only survivors on the whole of Earth — or will do when it sets off on the waters. All other life, human and animal, will be engulfed. We have nothing to fear from one solitary Ark, surely?'

'I agree,' another said urgently. 'It is our supreme chance to destroy what's left of the human race, and so wonderfully easy.'

'Far too easy,' the Leader responded, thinking. 'We might fall straight into a trap. Consider: If this being Kang is from another world, then his scientific knowledge must be high, and so must that of his contemporaries on his home planet. They must be watching Earth, and they will certainly see our arrival. Do you suppose they would remain passive whilst an unknown spaceship settles down to the planet that one of their number is trying to save? No. We might find ourselves outmatched by scientific skill, facing an armada from the void that would decimate us. Our best course is to study the other planets first.'

The rest of the expedition nodded, satisfied that their Leader had seen further than they had. They remained quiet whilst he adjusted the telescope and, presently, a view of mighty Jupiter girdled in his familiar cloud belts, loomed on the screen. Afterwards, by swift leaps in focus, the view leapt downwards through the whirling green clouds until the Jovian landscape merged into sight.

It was an inhospitable, brutal landscape upon which the alien scientists gazed. Colossal plateaux, low and vastly solid mountains, sullen liquid gas oceans clouded over with green vapours, and nowhere a sign of life. Not a shrub, not a tree, not a living thing. A world with an atmosphere of ammoniated-hydrogen, poisonous, desolate, and friendless beyond belief.

At the end of an hour of meticulous searching by the mighty telescope the Leader gave a sigh of relief. 'Apparently we have little to fear, my friends,' he said. 'My guess must have been wrong. There are not even cities below the surface, if the X-ray beams are to be credited.'

'In any case,' the pessimist pointed out,

'a creature from that world, with its ammonia-hydrogen atmosphere, could never breathe the Earth air.'

'That could be simply overcome by lung surgery,' the Leader retorted. 'However, we need not worry. That world is without doubt completely dead. Perhaps — one of the other worlds still further away?'

He adjusted the focusing mechanisms yet again and the inconceivable power of the telescope reached out beyond Jupiter to Saturn, then to Uranus, and finally Neptune. On the other worlds, however, the scenes differed but little from those of Jupiter. They were completely barren of life, still far too young in the scale of planetary evolution to contain intelligent life.

'Which means,' the Leader said at length, 'that this Kang is an Earthman, but I wish I knew his capabilities and could break him down.' He switched off the telescope and stood brooding.

The pessimistic alien spoke. 'There is nothing now to stop us going to Earth and destroying the Ark. Nobody will attempt to prevent us.'

'True. And yet — ' The Leader moved

uneasily. 'For some reason I feel most unsure,' he muttered. 'For instance, this Kang can hardly be outstanding among men, otherwise those around him would not have accepted him so easily. There may be others like him. Indeed, if he is an inhabitant of Mongolia, as he has said, then there are tens of thousands like him, so many indeed that we have not even attempted to learn their individual mental quotients. Somewhere on Earth there may be a race of beings who are supremely clever, of which this Kang is one. He calls himself a man of Mongolia, maybe because he resembles the people who live in that region, but that may be only to conceal his actual identity. If, somewhere, there is a hidden race of masterminds which our instruments haven't detected, we don't want to encounter them — and we would if we destroyed the Ark.'

'Then what do we do?' one of the aliens demanded, obviously becoming impatient. 'We are haggling and theorising and hitting on no definite plan, sire — '

'There is only one definite plan,' the Leader interrupted him. 'On that I am now decided. We must wait for the Deluge to cover the Earth and then see what happens. Even a master-race will emerge to the surface of the waters under those conditions and we will see what we face. Yes — that is it. Wait until the Deluge and then decide. In the meantime we will prepare a recorded message with all relevant co-ordinates and data on the Earth, ready to send by radio to our home planet. But we cannot transmit it until we are absolutely sure. Such a vast undertaking as a cosmic exodus will utterly deplete our home world's waning resources. We can only essay the one attempt. And we ourselves must not head for Earth until we are absolutely sure of what awaits us.'

'Agreed,' the others responded, and it was the sign that, as usual, they were ready to bow to the Leader's will.

★   ★   ★

On Earth, the door of the workers' dormitory had just closed behind Ox. Though the guards gave the usual 'lights out' order the men were all out of their bunks again immediately afterwards, gathering in a circle and listening to the persistent beating of the rain upon the roof.

With every passing second it seemed to increase its force. A slight wind had risen too, driving in blinding sheets against the windows. Outside it was swilling along the ground, dimly illumined by the battery-driven lamps at various points.

'Raining pretty badly,' Hoyle said, peering outside. 'I can well imagine that a few weeks of this will flood the world.'

'Then you've got a marvellous imagination,' Val commented dryly.

'Huh? How do you mean?'

'Great heavens,' Val exclaimed, 'you don't suppose that this is the Deluge, do you? It's only the first few drops of water compared to what is really to come! We get weather as bad as this on an ordinary winter day! No: just wait until the real thing arrives, and then you'll know the difference. We won't sit calmly here, believe me. We'll be scared to death!'

'What I want to know,' one of the workers snapped, 'is why we have to wait for Ox's orders! I say let's get to the Ark and have done with it!'

'He's right, Val!'

'What are we waiting for?'

'Now just a minute, boys — ' Val commenced to say, and then he paused and looked up sharply as a new sound came above the drumming of the rain. It was a rumbling roar, still afar off, like the approach of a mighty hurricane. The ground under the camp began to tremble. The downpour increased its drumming to a sudden shattering rattle over which it was difficult to shout.

'The Deluge!' Hoyle screamed. 'It's coming!'

Val glanced about him. 'Outside!' he ordered curtly. 'No time to wait for Ox.'

The men nearest the door tore it open and raced down the wooden steps. Out in the open air the roaring din sounded like a tempest-lashed ocean smashing against distant cliffs. Then, suddenly, came the Deluge — ! It came out of the moaning dark, a colossal roaring tide of water vomited from the crumbling sky. Instantly a vast Niagara crashed into the midst of the camp, hurling the men over, tearing down fences, crushing in the huts as though they were made of paper.

Val, caught in the raging tide, was slammed back into the crumbling camp. Water, cold and scum-laden, surged over his head. He came up gasping for breath to find himself fighting amidst fallen timbers and wreckage. Rain of incredible violence beat down upon his head, nearly forcing him under the swirling waters again.

'Help — please!' came a forlorn cry from nearby. 'Help me!'

Val fought his way round in a circle and was just in time to pull up a frantically struggling figure from under a heavy beam. It was Kang. The voice alone revealed it, for to see anything was next to impossible.

'Okay now?' Val panted, holding the little man's head over the water surface.

'Th — thank you, my friend,' the Mongolian choked. 'You are — are very strong. You don't know what you have done by — by saving me.'

'Done? Saved your life, that's all.' Val looked around anxiously in the screaming darkness. Above the noise of bubbling water and the whistle of descending rain there was another sound — the yelling voices of men and women.

Rita! He had completely forgotten her in the excitement of the moment.

'My wife!' he exclaimed in horror. 'I've got to find her. Here, Kang, hang onto this and — '

'The Ark!' Kang interrupted him. 'Look! The lights of the Ark! Accept my suggestion and head for the Ark before looking for your wife. It will be simpler. It has searchlights, remember. You'll never find your wife in this darkness and confusion.'

It was only Val's confidence in the strange little Mongolian which made him accept the suggestion — so he began to swim strongly towards the bobbing lights of the monster Ark as it floated on the tumbling water. Kang he helped along at his side.

It seemed obvious to Val that some of the men must have reached the Ark at a remarkable speed to have got it under way so quickly. Its searchlights were blazing across the waters now, picking out survivors. Everywhere there seemed to be bobbing heads and flailing arms. Men and women alike were battling desperately to reach the floating sanctuary.

It drew nearer, and the searchlights reflecting back from the water revealed a surprising sight. A giant figure stood in the main doorway, legs apart and revolver in hand, water pouring down his bristly head.

'I said the women first!' he bellowed, crashing his fist into the jaw of a man as he strove to reach the doorway. 'Get back and help the women. Drag 'em aboard! Lively now!'

He kept his feet with difficulty and watched like an eagle as the men in the water worked desperately to lift up the women prisoners as they floated close enough to be rescued.

'Ox!' Val panted. 'He got there first! I never could decide if he were a man or a monster: now I know he's got a spark of humanity somewhere under that armour-plating. *Hey, Ox! Hey!*'

7

Kang intervenes

At the shout, Ox swung round and peered into the searchlights' glare. Then his voice broke forth into a roar over the din of the rain.

'Come in here before the women and I'll shoot you down!'

'I've no intention of coming in,' Val shouted back, 'but what about little Kang here? He's sinking, and he's got brains enough worth saving.'

'Okay, up with him!' Ox reached down and pulled the little Mongolian upwards bodily. He uttered a brief gasp of thanks and then stumbled into the Ark's warm, lighted interior.

'That doesn't go for you, Turner!' Ox shouted. 'You've got plenty of muscle. Lend a hand with the women.'

'You seem to have got yourself into a nice safe position, Ox!' one of the swimming men bawled.

'Shut up, you. I got here first so I could ensure discipline. Got to do my duty. I saw the Flood coming and got things ready while you blockheads were wondering what to do. 'Sides, I've the women to protect with scum like you around. There'll be no funny business in this Ark, believe me! All right, let's have more of those women. No time to lose!' he finished with a bellow, as another huge rolling wave of water came thundering down into the chaos.

Val came up again with tortured lungs. This time all sign of the camp had gone. The world was a battering, roaring hell of rain, hurricane, and struggling bodies. The Ark still rode the storm undisturbed, its lighted portholes like watching eyes.

Time and again Val caught at a struggling woman prisoner and lifted her to the door where Ox seized her firmly and drew her up. Until at last Val grabbed the one woman he wanted most in the world — Rita, nearly at the point of exhaustion. With more care than hitherto he raised up her slack body.

'Easy with her, Ox,' he called up anxiously.

Ox swept her up: 'What's one woman more than another?' he asked sourly. 'Because she's your wife it doesn't make her extra-special — not to me. Keep working!'

Val smiled twistedly. He toiled on again, until at length it seemed that all the women who had survived the Flood were aboard.

'All right, you men,' Ox shouted at last. 'Come aboard — the old ones first.'

He stood aside, making no effort to lend a hand's turn as the men floundered up onto the steel flooring in the light and warmth. Val came last. He straightened up, breathing hard and dripping water.

Ox, his soaked uniform plastered to his massive body, flipped his gun to the silent Kang nearby.

'Kang, I nominate you as my deputy for the time being,' he said briefly. 'You've got more sense than all the rest of these pigs put together! See to it that nobody starts the Ark moving until I get back.'

Ox put his hands on his hips and gazed around him. 'I want a man with strong muscles and no fear to come with me,' he snapped out. 'I'm calling for a volunteer.'

'To do what?' Val questioned.

For answer Ox pointed through the driving rain. 'You see that solitary light across the water there? That's the headquarters on the rising ground overlooking the camp. Rutter and Angorstine, my superiors, are there. It is my duty to get them into this Ark, but the Ark cannot get that close. It'll take me and another strong man.' Ox paused, a sneering grin on his face. 'I know only one strong man here,' he added.

Val shook his head deliberately. 'Meaning me, I suppose? Nothing doing, Ox! Rutter and Angorstine between them caused all this havoc, and they can perish in it.'

Val turned away and Ox's cold eyes followed him. 'Whatever the causes, Turner, I've my duty to do. I don't personally like this hell we're going through any more than you do — but I swore allegiance to the Cause until the end. I still want a man,' he finished bitterly. 'Or are two men out there, no matter what they stand for, to drown?'

'Let 'em drown,' Val responded, sitting down on a crate and squeezing water out of his trouser legs.

'You can't do that, Val,' Rita said, coming over to him. 'If you can save two lives you should, even though they be the lives of your bitterest enemies.'

'Your wife is right, my friend,' murmured Kang, nodding slowly.

Val gave a grim look around him, then he got impatiently to his feet.

'All right,' he growled, 'but I can't see why the devil I'm so sentimental. Bring those two aboard this Ark and there'll never be peace any more.'

He tore off what remained of his shirt and then dived into the swirling scum outside. In another moment, like-wise stripped to the waist, Ox followed him. They swam powerfully, neither of them speaking, covering the mile of roaring waters and battering rain in fairly good time, stumbling at last up the sloping sides of the slowly vanishing island on which the headquarters building was situated.

Hardly had they both floundered through the headquarters doorway before Rutter came rushing to meet them with Angorstine behind him. Both of them were pale and obviously shaken.

'It's the Deluge, isn't it?' Rutter demanded.

'Which you started,' Val commented sourly. 'Only thing I'm sorry for is that the waters haven't caught up with you.'

'It is the Deluge, sir, yes,' Ox replied, saluting smartly. 'If you can swim there is safety a mile away, and if you cannot swim, I'll help you.'

'Why the hell didn't you bring a boat?' Rutter demanded.

'Impossible, sir — sorry. Conditions too rough. Prisoner Turner and I will give you a hand.'

'You will?' Rutter looked at the grim-faced Val. 'All you want, Turner, is an excuse to drown me!'

'Right,' Val agreed. 'But my better judgment won't prevail, I'm afraid. More your job than mine to kill in cold blood.'

'Why, you impudent — '

'No time to delay, sir,' Ox put in

165

urgently. 'The waters are rising fast.'

'I'll start immediately,' Angorstine interrupted, tearing off his coat. 'I can swim.'

He leapt for the door and prepared to dive, but Ox swung him around and caught his arm. With a smashing uppercut he sent Angorstine reeling. He lost his balance, pitched into the roaring tide, and vanished.

'That was murder!' Rutter screamed. 'You deliberately drowned him!'

'You should talk about murder,' Val remarked cynically.

'It was not murder,' Ox corrected. 'He tried to seek safety before — and without permission of — his superior. That is treason. Treason is punishable by death. I simply did my duty.'

Rutter stared blankly for a moment, astonished at Ox's relentless devotion to duty. Val remained silent, inwardly admiring Ox's unswerving notions on principles. Then Rutter apparently made up his mind. He tugged off his coat and lowered himself nervously into the water. Immediately Ox was on one side of him and Val on the other. Between them they got the gasping, terrified Dictator across that mile of thundering tempest, finally pushing him up into the Ark where he lay gasping on the floor.

Ox turned and slammed the doors, snatched up his gun, and then whirled round to face the grim survivors. 'Now remember this,' he barked. 'You too, Turner! Rutter is still our master. I am his aide now, since Angorstine is lost and I will follow his orders to the letter. When the waters subside the regime will continue, and as long as Miles Rutter lives we obey him. Understand?'

'With him shut up in here with us?' Hoyle roared. Like hell! He'll never live to see the waters subside, Ox. We'll get him somehow — and you too.'

Ox's eyes narrowed. 'Now you listen to me — all of you! The slightest attempt on Miles Rutter or myself, by man or woman, will be answered by death! Let that sink into your skulls. Now, you men, get to those oars and start rowing! You, Hoyle, get to the steering gear. You others pull over the partitions. Men in one end, women in the other. Step on it. Get yourselves dried out afterwards. You keep 'em quiet, Turner. I hold you responsible.'

Val nodded slowly. 'I'll do my best, Ox, because I'm satisfied that you've got manhood in you.' He looked sourly across at Rutter and then turned to get things in order.

Thanks to the foresight of Ox in forcing the prisoners to equip the Ark beforehand as fully as possible, there was no shortage of necessities: just the same he rationed everything, and for the first time in his life Rutter was obliged to accept rations with good grace. He was changed, too. He was in danger of his life every moment and knew it, despite the relentless vigilance that Ox maintained.

Val was pretty sure for his part that after a while the people would leave Rutter unmolested as long as he kept quiet, but that they would ever again bow to his leadership was a debatable point. In fact there was no doubt whatever about the answer. It would be a flat and uncompromising negative.

★　★　★

The aliens were anxiously surveying Earth, which, with the Deluge, had now become little better than a hydrosphere. The view on their telescopic screen was of a world completely sheathed in tumbling cloud belts, and when the X-ray beams penetrated through the veil they settled upon endlessly rolling waters, deserted except for one solitary Ark steadily riding the Flood.

'Just as well that we did not leave too soon for Earth,' the Ruler commented, as these scenes persisted day after day. 'We can do nothing with a world of water in which only the mountain peaks seem to have survived. We must at least wait until the waters subside.'

'What of the Ark?' one of the aliens asked quietly.

'Apparently it contains the only surviving life on the planet. Do you still believe we should hold off from destroying it?'

'Attack it,' another insisted. 'We can reach Earth in a matter of hours and blast that object from the face of the waters, then indeed Earth will be empty — ready for us to take possession of when the waters have receded.'

The Leader did not answer. He was looking fixedly at the instrument that registered mental-frequency. It was still trained on far-distant Kang, as it had been at the time when the Ruler had failed to read the Mongolian's brain-energy, but now the needle had mysteriously reacted and stood at just over fifty per cent, a rating far above that of any other thinking Earthman.

'Look!' the Leader exclaimed in amazement, pointing. 'At last our mystery friend Kang is registering! Why? What has unsealed his mind to us, I wonder?'

'Of what concern is that?' an alien demanded. 'His mind can now be read — or we can hear what he is saying, perhaps?'

'Better to read his mind,' the Leader replied quickly, and flinging himself to the instruments he went to work rapidly. Sensitive beams probed immediately across the gulf, and at last pinpointed Kang. Meanwhile others of the aliens manipulated the telescope until they had its X-ray focus trained on Kang himself.

He was not talking. He was not doing anything, in fact. He sat in a corner of the Ark, surrounded by men and women, his eyes apparently closed in concentration.

'An excellent opportunity to learn something,' the Leader said, glancing at the screen. Then he turned his attention to the complicated loudspeaker, which, by means of transformers, convened the thoughts of distant Kang into vibrations. In actual audible sound they did not make sense, being merely a series of vari-toned notes, but to the sensitive brains of the aliens each vibration registered clearly as a thought, which they were able to read as easily as a radio receiver picks up radio waves and transforms them into intelligible sound. It was, to them, as if they were gazing into a series of mind-pictures, bright and clear.

Silent, the aliens stood, their eyes closed, their beings concentrated on the task of 'reading' the brain of the mystery man so far away, and the more they saw into his mind the more disquieted they became.

There were views of a titanic city, apparently below ground and artificially lighted, populated by industrious beings — men and women — who exactly resembled Kang. The views of the city, from various angles, frequently dissolved and were replaced by mighty power rooms, dwarfing in expanse and equipment anything that the aliens possessed. There were glimpses of enormous atom-projectors, obviously intended for defensive purposes; there were storage-hangars in which stood at least a thousand space-machines abreast, all of them massively equipped with armament. Laboratories by the score, power-rooms, whole sections of the city given over to armaments so varied that they could not be assessed. There were views of robots hundreds of thousands of them, marching to the orders of an Unknown. The one thought running across it all was that Kang was the Master of all this, the head of an underground city somewhere. It might be on Earth: it might be on some far distant world. Kang's mind pictures did not reveal the true facts.

Then suddenly these incredible scenes faded and were replaced by a mental image of Kang himself — small, brown, smiling inscrutably. It seemed as though he spoke, but actually it could only have been his thoughts, forming nonetheless into words that the aliens interpreted into their own language.

'You, inhabitants of another stellar system, have just observed a few glimpses of the scientific power which I, Kang, control at a remote quarter of this world of Earth. Do you imagine that a cataclysm like the Deluge could possibly destroy such science as ours, or the people responsible for it? No. And rest assured, you inhabitants of another planet, that if you come to this world of ours you will be instantly destroyed by powers infinitely greater than any you possess. Myself and my contemporaries are fully aware of your activities, and also of your intention to destroy or deplete the peoples of Earth so that your race might take over this world for your own uses. Hence my warning now! Keep away, or be vapourised into pure energy. The choice is yours.

'I have, up to this point, set a neutral field around my brain so that you could not penetrate my thoughts, but now I have temporarily lifted it, to send this communication. As scientists you are at least entitled to know the answer to the problem that baffled you. I would repeat my warning — Keep away! If you must die, then die with honour on your own decadent world.'

The communication faded, and though Kang's image remained on the telescopic screen his thoughts were again neutralised and the mental-energy instrument had dropped its needle to zero once more. The Leader turned, switched off the instruments and the telescope and then looked at his comrades.

'You received that communication?' he asked.

The faces of the aliens were despondent. It was the pessimistic one who finally answered.

'Yes, sire, the communication reached us clearly enough, and though you have often upbraided me for always considering the unknown factor I feel obliged to say, in my own defence, that we have indeed encountered it in Kang.'

'I apologise, my friend,' the Leader said frankly. 'You have proven completely right. In Kang we see the end of our ambitions. We know now that he is capable of seeing us, perhaps even of hearing us. We could never go to Earth under such conditions. We could never face the monstrous engines his mentality permitted us to view. We saw there an applied science infinitely ahead of ours.'

'Which puzzles me,' another remarked, musing. 'We have examined Earth thoroughly, and have never even glimpsed a city such as we saw mirrored in those mind-pictures. Where is it? Where can it be hidden? We have studied Earth's surface, and below its surface, but have never discovered anything of particular interest.'

'We hardly would if the inhabitants of that city were aware of us,' the Leader shrugged. 'They would prevent any light-waves leaving it: hence we would not see it. Such scientists as these followers of Kang appear to be would certainly guard their secrets from watching interplanetary eyes.'

'If Kang did not speak the truth? If the mind-pictures he presented were but myths, contrived by his imagination, what then?'

For a long time the Ruler considered, then he shook his head. 'There, my friend, we are in a quandary. I admit that Kang may have projected mental images that are pure imagination, in which case there is actually nothing on that Earth but the Ark and those within it, but, on the other hand, he may have been projecting the truth. We cannot afford the risk in case the latter should be the case. Imagination or otherwise we are defeated.'

There was silence as the logic of the statement penetrated. Then the Leader moved in a gesture of resignation. 'So be it then, my friends. We and our race are a proud and brilliant people. We have tried to conquer the only world discovered so far that was suitable for our type of life, and have failed. We must bow to the superior intelligence, or imagination, of this creature known as Kang.'

'And now?' the pessimist asked.

'Now? What else is there to do but

inform our people by radio that Earth is unsuitable for migration — that they must await the messages of the other probes still travelling through space.'

'And what of ourselves?' the pessimist questioned.

'Our mission has failed.' The Leader bowed his head. 'We must set a return course, back to our own dying world. Prepare the suspended animation cabinets.'

★ ★ ★

Whatever spare time he could snatch, Val spent with Rita. Through the portholes of the Ark, as it was rowed onwards day after day by relays of men, visible in the dim daylight which filtered through the midnight clouds, there was nothing but a waste of water. It would have needed a world trip to fully grasp the extent of the catastrophe the G-Bombs had started.

The heavens in their disgorge of waters had refilled the ocean beds and hammered their unimaginable weight and volume into the land as well. Coasts had eroded, hills slipped down, ravines burst asunder under mighty cataracts. And not even now was the Deluge ended. The clouds were so low they nearly touched the surface of the water. There was wind, too, an incessant moaning gale that howled dismally over the grey expanses.

'I wonder,' Rita said thoughtfully, towards the close of the fifth day, 'where we are going to end this drifting?'

It was Ox who answered her. 'Where we started! I gave orders for us to move constantly in a circle so that we might still be in the region of Britain or Europe when the waters subside.' He glared across at the helmsman and steadily rowing oarsmen in their seats. 'That's what you have done, isn't it?' he snapped.

The helmsman in particular looked uncomfortable and kept silent.

'Answer!' Ox roared.

To everybody's surprise it was Kang who spoke next. As usual he was crouched on his little stool in a corner, a wizened gnome of a creature with a mystical smile.

'I can answer for the helmsman, my

178

friend. He is obeying my orders for a course, not yours.'

Ox purpled. 'What! Those orders were given to me by Leader Rutter! By what right — '

'Let him speak,' Rutter himself interrupted curtly.

'But, Leader, it is treason when — '

'It is not treason when I was concerned for the safety of everybody aboard this Ark,' Kang interrupted. He turned and looked around him on the assembly. 'Perhaps this is as good a time as any to explain one or two points.'

'What points?' Ox demanded.

'Patience, Captain, please. In the first place I think you should know that the Cataclysm which has descended on Earth was not entirely a natural occurrence. It was brought about deliberately by the inhabitants of a planet in another solar system.'

Everybody waited, some gaping. Kang continued, quite undisturbed.

'I come from a race who have mastered the ultimate secrets of mind. Just which race I will explain in a moment. First let me tell you that by mind force alone we discovered an alien plot to conquer this world without setting foot upon it. The thought processes of these aliens were laid bare to us in our Contemplation Chambers. We saw how they intended to plant a valuable secret in the mind of one Jonas Glebe and use him as a pawn in the cosmic chess game. The other pawn was you — Miles Rutter.'

'Me?' Rutter started and then projected his chin. 'Nobody uses me as a pawn!' he retorted. 'I think you're drivelling!'

'Do you?' Kang smiled slightly. 'Believe me, you have been only a tool. You gained world domination not from your own initiative, or even ambition, but because the desire was willed into you by expert scientists a million miles away. However, they are not so expert that they can handle mind projections as simply as I can. Nor am I unique. Many of my race are masters of mind — '

'Who are you?' Val broke in. 'Where on this planet does there exist a race of mind experts? I've never heard of them.'

'Then you have never heard of Tibet.'

As the men and women started in surprise Kang continued: 'Tibet is noted for its mystics, and for its mastery over the physical laws. I was singled out to venture into the outer world — along with forty-nine others of my race — and gather together the survivors of the Deluge. We of Tibet have led a sheltered life of mental achievement for many generations. We knew of, but were not concerned with, the wars of the outer world. We only moved at all when we realised alien domination was impending which might present an ultimate menace to us. On the scientific side we were aware of the action of the G-Bombs and consequent evaporation of Earth's moisture, which could only result in a second Deluge. Our geographical prognosticators showed that all Tibet, and our sheltered kingdom included, would be completely inundated by the Deluge to come.'

By now all signs of opposition to the little Mongolian had ceased. He glanced about him with his oblique eyes and then continued:

'It was clear to us that nearly all the

inhabitants of the Earth would be drowned in the Flood, but it might be possible to save a few — a few who could at least rebuild a better civilisation with our assistance. We had no wish to live in the world alone: such an occurrence would be detrimental since the human race might die out completely. Some had got to be saved and brought to safety until the Flood should subside. Over it all hung the threat of the aliens. They waited — to pounce.'

Kang gave his inscrutable smile. 'The aliens — so our mental reading of them told us — knew all we were doing and could even read the thoughts of most people. They could not, however, read my thoughts or those of my race because if you are proficient in the art, it is simple to blank your mind and prevent thoughts being read. I maintained this attitude until recently when I decided I must make the supreme move in the cosmic chess-game. Briefly I allowed my mind to be read, knowing the aliens would be ready for it, and allowed them to digest the most amazing tissue of scientific visions ever created. They believe there exists on this world such terrific weapons that they dare not try and come here and wipe out the survivors.'

'And such power does not exist?' Val asked listening intently.

'No. Only in the imagination. We of Tibet are mental experts, not physical scientists, but the aliens have been convinced by my imaginings that they will be decimated if they try and attack or overpower us. Purely a checkmate move, my friends. They may guess I am bluffing, but they cannot ever prove it. So, held out by the threat of disaster, they will keep away. Incidentally, Mister Turner, you thought your idea of an Ark was spontaneous. It was not. I willed the idea into your mind. You found a way of making an Ark so easily that it astonished you. In other parts of the world my fellow-thinkers will have given mental orders for Arks to be created. There may not be many but there will certainly be some, each Ark carrying survivors. In these Arks lies the nucleus of a new civilization — better, wider, finer than any before.'

'And yet Tibet is, I take it, under water?' Ox sneered. 'Not very effectual, my friend, are you?'

Kang turned to him. 'Tibet is under water, yes, but not the particular intellectual sects who formerly inhabited it. Tibet is within easy reach of Everest, the highest point on Earth. We have complete knowledge of how to scale that mountain and know every foot of its surface. Once we knew the Deluge would come we removed everything of value to that mountain's highest caves. In there, shut off from the winds and water, lies the oldest and newest science in the world — metaphysical science, of which we are consummate masters. We shall train all survivors in the art. Eventually, one day, only beings of mind shall populate this Earth.'

Kang's voice trailed off and there was the look of a visionary in his strange eyes. Ox's powerful voice was a distinct jolt when it boomed forth.

'Then you have been instructing this helmsman to drive towards Everest all this time? To India?'

'To the second Ararat,' Kang conceded.

'You shan't do it!' Rutter cried, leaping to his feet. 'I am the ruler here! I don't believe one word of this chess-game with aliens you speak of. I don't believe one word about a race of mind-scientists. There can be no new regime as long as I rule — and rule I shall until the end. I'll break you, Kang, and your science — just as I have broken everything else that stood in my way.'

'Except your neck,' Val growled.

Kang remained undisturbed. He did not even move. His deliberate sleepy voice came forth again. 'The fly does not hurt the elephant no matter how hard it kicks,' he commented. 'You are the last of a race of material egomaniacs who will soon lie rotting beneath the waters.'

'You forget me,' Ox remarked. 'I swore allegiance, and I have been — and still am — true to it.'

'For that all praise is due you,' Kang answered. 'For the Cause you worship you are to be pitied — deeply pitied. What is left of it beyond this warped, blustering creature of useless vanity? You,

185

Rutter, will not stand for a second against the metaphysical powers of Tibet. You are foresworn to destruction.'

Rutter sat down again, slowly. There was a certain rock-like calm about Kang, an unshakable conviction of supreme power. Without haste, without even a raised word, he drove his points home.

'In other words,' Rutter said at last, 'I am being considered as ruler while we are on this Ark, only to be destroyed by mental science when we reach this Everest Ararat?'

'We do not take life, Rutter. That would be contrary to the laws of mental advance. We are not murderers and we are not avengers. You will enter with us to live your life quietly as long as your conscience will permit you but you will no longer rule: be assured of that. You will have time — many years maybe — to wrestle with yourself if you wish it.'

Ox opened his mouth to speak, and then closed it again.

Rutter was staring straight in front of him as the full weight of Kang's words sank in. By slow degrees the assembled people, Rutter included, began to see what was proposed as punishment for the would-be ruler of the world. He proposed freedom — freedom in which to search his conscience, freedom to remember, but with power forever snatched from his grasp. A snake without its sting. It was calm, inexorable retribution, with its inescapable hint of Oriental inhumanity.

For five more days the Ark travelled onwards under the power of the oars, carried too by tremendous wind force.

The rain continued. Hardly anybody slept during the period. They were mainly at the ports staring out over the watery waste or else talking amongst themselves. Now and again they caught glimpses of distant lights bobbing on the waves — lights that could only belong to other Arks moving towards a common goal, Arks which the preoccupied aliens had failed to detect.

Until at last, days later, something loomed out of the drab, rain-lashed greyness perhaps three miles ahead. It was a titanic rocky spire, a mountain thrusting up into girdling clouds. There was an immediate rush to the windows to study it.

'Everest!' somebody shouted.

'No,' Kang corrected quietly. 'A mountain in the lower Himalayas. Everest is — there!'

At that moment the Ark turned slightly and the astounding vision burst full upon the sight. For a moment the raging rain thinned a little and the awe-inspiring mass of Mount Everest itself loomed in view, rearing to the darkness with waters dimly visible ploughing and churning around its invincible mass. Here and there bobbed the lights of the other Arks.

'You shan't do it!' Rutter cried suddenly. 'You shan't take me there, Kang! You shan't take me to be looked at and pointed to as a specimen.'

He broke off and picked up a chair, whirling it in an arc towards the little Mongolian. Halfway in its flight, the chair dropped as Kang's calm eyes met the inflamed ones of the former dictator. Rutter fell slowly back towards the wall, pulling at his lips. The steady, inexorable gaze followed him.

'Not there — ' Rutter whispered, drooling. 'Not there — '

'Leader, what is the matter?' Ox caught, at him fiercely and forced him to stand up straight. 'Leader, what is wrong? Command me! I am still here to obey! I will force these scum to do — '

Rutter looked at Ox dully. 'Bombs — Send in Mister Glebe — We'll sink 'em deep down, Standish! Deep down! Where is Standish? *Standish!*'

'Easy, Leader — easy,' Ox panted, staring fixedly at a trickle of saliva running from Rutter's undisciplined lips.

Rita turned away, sickened. Val caught her head on his shoulder, watching intently. He turned suddenly to Kang.

'Kang, did you — ?' Amazement stopped him.

The Mongolian only smiled — inscrutably. It seemed to verify Val's belief that the mind-scientist had used his superior intellectual power to snap once and for all the reason of the former dictator.

'Where's Standish?' Rutter repeated, gazing unseeingly through Ox. 'Where — where is he? It's so dark in here — '

'Somebody, knock him out!' screamed Hoyle. 'He's gone crazy!'

Ox shook himself as though getting rid of a vast unbelief. Very deliberately he tugged out his gun, levelled it then fired. He stood watching as Rutter's gross body sank slowly to the floor and became still.

The silence of the assembly was complete. Only the howling wind and beating rain made any noise at all. Everybody watched, motionless, as Ox lifted the dead body on his broad shoulder and carried it to the rear window. He forced the frame open, eased the corpse outside, and dropped it onto the waters. Then he turned back and gave a final salute. He fired one shot from his gun into the air and then laid the weapon carefully on a side table. This done he turned, his face set. 'The regime I obeyed is ended,' he announced. 'I swore my allegiance until death. The good soldier knows when it is his duty to surrender.'

Before anybody could grasp his intention he turned back to the window, wriggled through it, and was gone. The glass slammed shut, but by the time

everybody had rushed to it the waste of ocean outside was dark and empty.

'He killed himself,' Val whispered. 'The crazy, duty-drunk fool!'

'No — a good soldier,' Kang corrected. Then he looked towards the gleaming mountain ramparts coming nearer. 'There is the foundation of a new world, my friends,' he added, 'wherein the frailties and lusts of Mankind shall be forever swallowed up.'

THE END

MIRACLE MAN
THE MULTI-MAN
THE RED INSECTS
THE GOLD OF AKADA
RETURN TO AKADA
GLIMPSE
ENDLESS DAY